Tides of DESIRE

A Christmas Romance

TRACY SUMNER

TIDES OF DESIRE

Learn more about the author and her books at
Tracy-Sumner.com

Cover Design and Interior Format

To all the readers who asked for Caleb's story.
I love you guys!

CHAPTER ONE

Outer Banks, NC
December 1899

CHRISTMAS WAS A SPLENDID TIME to be in love.

And the worst time to be *out* of it.

This was Caleb Garrett's verdict as he shouldered past a couple leaving Scoggins's Mercantile, their gazes locked on each other as they shared the *look*. If he judged by nothing *but* his brothers' ridiculously happy marriages, the way they communicated without saying a word and how conflicted, how lonely, it made him feel lately to witness it, he would have to say his verdict was lacking in holiday cheer, but was, nonetheless, accurate.

He passed Christabel's restaurant without pausing to stop for coffee, conversation. Or more, in the back bedroom he'd once considered his own.

Because times and people changed.

An agreed-upon, handled-like-adults change.

The tinny sound of a piano skated past on a salt-laden gust bitter enough to make his skin sting, the lively tune perfect for the season.

Tightening the soiled length of linen circling his bicep, he grimaced as a painful jolt shot down his arm. Carolers had strolled past his warehouse every evening this week, until he'd been forced to barricade himself in his workshop with his phonograph—a birthday gift from his brother, Noah, that he unabashedly and quite surprisingly loved. While the group sang with boundless glee outside and Joplin let it loose inside, Caleb had used his incarceration to finish the Chesapeake sharpie design for a New England boatbuilder. A brilliant little skiff that would scoot right over the waves without a tremor if things went as planned.

So, he guessed he'd give the carolers some credit.

Although he still thought love and Christmas did not go together. Or didn't *have* to, as everyone seemed to think they should.

Halting before a house the color of a dirty sock, he noted the cracked foundation, ballast stone at its best fifty years ago; a tattered cypress shake roof that had to be leaking. Drab, but holding a lovely spot right on the bay, where the smell of the marsh was deep and pungent, an eternal balm to his soul. He gave the stained cloth circling his arm another tug. No repairs done on this place because there was no man to do them. And according to rumor, no money to hire one. Caleb stubbed the heel of his boot across the warped porch step before he stepped on it, watched a seagull sail past and questioned if he could forgo this visit. Handle this crisis on his own with a poultice and some of that miracle salve Elle had given him that might be dried up because he'd left the top off.

Because...Macy Dallas, *for the love of God*.

From beneath his makeshift bandage, a crimson bead trickled down his arm and over his wrist. A drop the exact color of the holly hanging on every one of his sister-in-law Savannah's new gas streetlamps hitting the faded porch board as if to say: *no, indeed, stitches are required*.

He had a choice: the lady doctor or one of his brothers. His inquisitive, concerned, protective, interfering brothers. Although the thought of *her* gave his belly an unwelcome twist. Engaged his cock, too, if he were being honest.

How weak is man, he concluded and sent the sign hanging next to the door—Elinor Macy Dallas, Medical Doctor—into a wild swing. The disparity brought an unwelcome smile to his face. The house was decaying, but the sign brand spanking new, as was the doctor. The nervous belly-twist when he got near Miss Dallas, not so much.

He'd been dealing with that for a while now.

Counting to five, he blew out a fierce breath and knocked. Cock *definitely* engaged by the mere thought of her, which irritated him for no good reason.

The second knock was not gentle.

The door opened and she emerged from a gaslight glow, her eyes the exact sapphire of Martin Tisdale's lumberyard skiff. Those eyes widened before the shadows pulled her back in and concealed what she thought of him showing up at this hour on her front porch. A haunting chorus of sound drew them closer when neither moved a muscle, released a breath. Waves slapping the wharf, the frantic call of a heron in search of food, and in the faint distance, the rub and grind of a whaling ship anchoring at the dock.

Macy stepped back, took a long look. At his arm, the bandage, the blood dripping on her porch landing. A leisurely assessment that thawed him from the inside out, though he tried mightily to contain it. He started running calculations in his head, stern to rudder, transom to coaming, plank to bow, telling himself this was *not* the time. Not the *woman*. The numbers dissipated like mist as she nodded once and turned, expecting him to follow. Pulse racing, he closed the door behind him and leaned against it, wishing like hell his nervousness was due to her relative inexperience as a doctor instead of what he feared was making him jittery.

When he wasn't, never had been, jittery around women.

"Mr. Garrett?" she called, having gone down the hallway and into a room he assumed was her office. When he got there, he found her calmly removing supplies from a bruised glass cabinet, arranging them next to a chair he supposed she wanted him to settle in. Gauze, needle, thread, cotton balls, bottle of this, metal tin of that. He sat as the pungent smell of camphor and soap enveloped him. Oh, and her scent underneath it all. Something light, floral, though he couldn't peg what flower exactly. A feminine bit of nonsense he'd have expected from Savannah or Elle, but not Macy. Not this smart as a whip, capable, tough little thing. Barely reached his shoulder but with him sitting, unnervingly eye-to-eye.

She cleaned the needle, then began threading it with the steadiest regard he could imagine when you were set to poke it through skin. "Couldn't go to Doctor Leland after punching him in the face, I gather."

Caleb sat back with an indrawn sigh, alcohol stinging his nostrils and zipping to the back of his throat. *Fine*, he'd go there if confessing past transgressions was what it took to get medical attention. "My brother, Noah, came back to town after ten years gone. Without a word gone, don't know if you're dead or alive gone, and the town doctor felt *he* should be the first one to tell me. Let's just say I took it poorly. With my fist poorly."

Macy placed the threaded needle on a towel and grasped the ends of his ruined sleeve and yanked, ripping the material to his shoulder. His eyes met hers, and he couldn't help but notice the flush firing her cheeks, the first hint that she might be as disconcerted as he was. The image of her tearing off the rest of his clothing roared through his willing mind.

"Maybe he was heartbroken," she offered. "Tends to send one into a tailspin, doesn't it?"

"How should I know?" Though everyone in town presumed he knew *exactly* what being heartbroken felt like. "You didn't grow up here, but Elle and Noah were legendary. Leland was a fool to get in between that."

"Legendary," she murmured, her gaze skating away from him.

He shrugged, not able to hide his hiss of pain. He didn't know how to answer for what was and always had been, what he'd never actually experienced himself, so he observed in silence as she cut material into one long strip and a few smaller ones, the needle he wasn't looking forward to piercing his skin winking in the gaslamp's brilliant glow. She moved like a dancer, he decided, the most economical but to his mind elegant shifts and bends.

Her clothing definitely didn't contribute to her appeal. Her dress was plain and serviceable. But tucked so agreeably around each gentle curve it could have been a fancy ballgown and not looked any better. He followed it to her toes and back, wondering in a forbidden part of his mind what her lithe little body would feel like spread beneath him.

"There isn't glass in there, I'm hoping." She pointed the scissors at his wound.

He shook his head, forcing the image of her wrapped around him *and enjoying it* to the basement of his mind. "No shards from a bottle, Doc, if that's what you're asking. A brawl didn't bring me here."

She raised a brow. "Did I imply you were involved in an altercation?"

"No, but you considered it."

She clicked her tongue against her teeth and

stepped in to wash the injury, her touch light but efficient. "Excuse me, I—"

"Can't blame you. I'm known for it." When she continued to stare without commenting, her hand poised over his arm, he added, "Using my fists. Hitting first, thinking later." He paused, flexing those fists while trying to figure how to explain. "But I'm trying to improve my behavior. That's the way Savannah puts it anyway."

A smile raced across Macy's face. Like lightning, it lit her up. She tilted her head at the end of her amusement and dropped the blood-stained rag in a basin at her side, the move sending her hair into her face. It was loose, which it usually wasn't. A flaxen waterfall down her back, caressing her cheeks. Maybe those silken strands were where the floral scent was coming from, digging beneath his skin harder than the mast edge that had sliced him up had.

She grasped the needle, flicked her eyes his way as she gave the thread a hard tug. "I have liquor if you require fortification."

He settled back, steeling himself because he honestly didn't love needles. And he'd had enough encounters to know. But he just shook his head. Wagged his fingers. *Go on.*

Be a man, Caleb Eli, he heard his father say. *Toughen up.* He felt the shove accompanying the statement like his father was standing in the room with him. It was a misplaced memory. An unpleasant one. Distressing, when he'd fought his entire life to leave that bastard behind.

Though she had no idea, Macy Dallas was dealing with more than a shoulder wound today.

The first prick of steel beneath his skin was the worst, and he swallowed, allowing himself to get used to the sting. As she whispered soft words of comfort and worked her magic, he gazed out the lone window, where he could just see a slice of the ocean. She'd left it open and a weighty winter breeze slipped in, solace for his heated skin. The moon had arrived in a pitch sky, shooting a silvery strip across the carpet he was tempted to drag his boot through. "That degree all nice and tied up, right, Doc? I don't want some"—he breathed through a swift jolt of pain—"raggedy scar after this because you haven't completed your training."

Her hand tensed on his arm as she released what sounded like an irritated exhalation. "I found a facility willing to do post-graduate instruction, so rejoice, your scar will only be moderately ugly." She gently probed the wound, scrutinized, her body drawing so close his breath caught. "That's where I was the past year. Residency. Philadelphia. The position ended, and I returned to help Savannah with a public health campaign. Also, honestly, not many hospitals employ female doctors. And if they do, the positions are very competitive. Until then, it's private practice." He turned his head in time to see her swallow tightly. "Even here, where there is great need, I may not have patients. Or not many. And it's just me, so…" She pressed her lips together. "We'll see."

His heart did a dive as he sat there wondering

what to say and wishing he didn't want to touch her so desperately. Because touching would get them nowhere, especially if he couldn't separate desire from compassion. And at the moment, he couldn't. "I'm a patient," he said to smooth over the awkwardness, sympathy winning the battle.

When she finished, she snipped the thread and passed her thumb over a very neat set of stitches. He'd counted ten but might have missed a couple with her scent twisting his thoughts.

A low hum was her only reply as she opened a tin of horrific-smelling ointment and dabbed it on with a light touch. A sure touch, which didn't surprise him. A lock of her hair brushed his cheek, and he closed his eyes, settling into the contact. It had been months, a year almost, since he'd experienced anything even remotely soothing.

"It takes time," she told him as she applied a dressing, covering it with a length of snowy cotton that wouldn't stay pristine long, "to build a practice. They'll trust me at some point, or as is evidenced tonight, they'll have to."

Most of the people in Pilot Isle had their heads up their asses, but how could he admit that? Truth was, he'd be sitting in Magnus Leland's office, even though he despised the man, if he *and* his brothers hadn't gotten into it with him on more than one occasion. Personally, he had no qualms about going to a female doctor. Hell, he'd practically taken a college course in women's freedom in the past year, what with Noah *and* Zach marrying patriots for the cause. He'd even painted signs for Savannah's last campaign to gain the vote, God help him.

His problem wasn't championing the radical females in his family but, rather, working through the sizable infatuation he had with the lady doctor currently stitching him up.

"A position somewhere will come around, I'm sure," he said when she'd completed the procedure and stood there, seemingly lost about what to do next. He'd seen her work a shipwreck a few months back, about the most ghastly business there was. She'd bandaged and soothed and buried, doing what needed to be done without complaint. Never a hint she was somewhere she shouldn't be, standing among the debris and the bodies.

It wasn't only intelligence she had going for her.

She was beautiful in...he wasn't sure how to describe it, in a most *unusual* way. Not the standard package: pretty face, agreeable figure. No, something in the way she looked at a person, or at least the way she looked at *him*, set her apart from every woman he'd ever known. Her eyes a rolling sea of knowledge, as vast as the one he sailed his skiffs over. Made a man want to explore, dive in and not look back. He was fine to jump in without thinking about it too awful much. Not like Noah and Zach, who'd dragged their heels until their women had up and left them.

Only...Macy Dallas. He ducked his head. *Not going to happen.*

She was leagues above anyone he'd even *considered* being attracted to. Too good for him by far. Anyway, she was leaving as soon as she found a hospital to employ her. His heart wouldn't be able to take abandonment of such magnitude, even if negotiated and intentional.

A punch he knew was coming.

As he sat there pondering how lovely she smelled and how he could do nothing about it, she took a step back. Smoothed her hand over her skirt. Fingered the tin of ointment, the bottle of alcohol, rearranged her cotton strips. While he was beginning to suspect she was going to—

"About that night. At the social. I should apologize."

Oh, Lord, he thought and let his head drop back to the chair with a thunk. There was a crack in her ceiling wide enough to put his pinky in. He wished he could crawl into it. "You did. Twice that I recall."

"I followed a perilous impulse after imbibing at least three glasses of—"

"Big words are wasted on me, Doc. Save them for the quilting circle."

"I had no idea she was there. That you were connected to someone. I can only be thankful Miss Connery didn't say a word after finding us. When I'm the depraved one, which I've never, *ever* been." She huffed a breath, squeezed the life from a cotton ball. "And I attend that frivolous quilting circle so I can practice my stitches!"

"If I made a solemn vow"—he looked up, waited until her gaze met his, wanting this information to sink in and hold like an anchor on the ocean floor—"you had nothing, and I mean *nothing*, to do with what happened between me and Christabel, can we agree to never discuss this again?"

Those wondrous eyes of hers sparked, flooding the room blue.

So, she did have a temper. Well, good, because so did he.

"Is this foul mood because I kissed you, Mr. Garrett? Or because you took a sharp dig to a vital body part?"

He was on his feet fast enough to send pain slicing down his arm. "It's because…" He looked away, clenched his jaw to keep from saying more. This time, thankfully, it was Noah's voice circling his mind and not his father's. *Think first, Cale.* With a sigh, he met Macy's gaze even though he didn't want to. Because he was an honest man if nothing else.

But then, *dammit*, he couldn't quite admit: *It's because you get to me, Miss Dallas, apart from that impassioned but brief kiss.* Because the sentiment needed polishing, like that dink in the hull of Fred Sanderlin's skiff. He'd smoothed that thing over until he and Fred forgot it was even there to begin with. And starting a conversation with *because you get to me* was all about jagged edges.

"It wasn't an impressive kiss," she murmured, circling a length of material around her hand and jerking until her skin shone white. "Not in the grand scheme of things. Not enough to cause irreparable damage."

As she fidgeted with the rag, her gaze drifting

around the room, he studied her. The kiss had been fleeting, yes, but *blinding*. A kiss to kill. With all the power of what *could be* hidden behind a just-out-of-the-gate effort. Amusing, maybe, because wasn't life funny even when you didn't want it to be? But you couldn't hide that much heat even under layers of naïveté. Unimpressive, huh? Her fingers had been tangled in his hair and his rising to do the same by the end of it. He'd had her backed against the wall in the assembly hall's cloakroom, heading to doing God knows what before they'd been discovered. Imagine if he'd had time to get his bearings, be a touch creative about the thing.

Anyway, the problem wasn't the kiss. It was his *compulsion*. Watching her worry on her gorgeous bottom lip while wanting to comfort, soothe, step in and make it better. Improve the situation. *Goddamnit*. The Garretts were known for protecting their own and, oh, did it look like he was staying true to course.

He murmured his thanks and was across the room and down the hallway before he followed the irrational impulses zipping through his mind, his body.

"Mr. Garrett," she called, right on his heels. "*Caleb*."

Sighing loud and long, he paused on her porch, the tattered ends of his shirt fluttering around his waist. Tapping her sign with his knuckle, he sent it swinging with a squeak. "Thanks for sewing me up, Doc. Send me the bill, will you?" he asked, his breath frosting the air. "Go back in. It's freezing out here, and you're not dressed for it. And, truthfully, neither am I."

"I'm sorry for the kiss, is what I wanted to convey."

His gaze jumped to hers as frustration raced through him. "Well, I'm not. How about that?"

Her mouth opened, closed. She shook her head, clearly stunned. Damn, those eyes of hers illuminated the night like a flare over the ocean. "I don't understand."

"Lucky for me," he threw over his shoulder as he stalked down the shell-paved path leading away from her doorstep, "you don't have to."

CHAPTER TWO

THE FIRST THING MACY HAD noticed was his kindness.

Hidden beneath layer upon layer of muscle and a rather determined stare, he presented, all told, an intimidating exterior. People would not utter kindness and Caleb Garrett in the same breath, not unless they really knew him. Took the time to do a thorough examination. She tapped the pencil against her bottom lip. The fact he had a reputation as a brawler was not surprising, because he looked the part. Yet, the night of the shipwreck, amidst a world of chaos and horror, he had cared for the fallen with compassion and a gentle regard she had not expected from a man. Had never experienced *with* a man.

In fact, she had experienced the opposite.

She swept her hand over the leaflet on women's health services Savannah had asked her to review without seeing a line of text. Without hearing a word as the women's league meeting buzzed around her, filling every darkened corner of Savannah's cozy parlor.

His eyes were the second thing she'd noticed, piercing gunmetal in a slice of moonlight skipping off the sea. The Garrett grays, they called them, because the three brothers shared them. Caleb's *were* gray, yes. Deeply, absorbingly so, but they were not exactly like Zach's and Noah's. And she'd taken the time to analyze. A bit of covert research, when, as a doctor, research was a gift. His not only had streaks of molten brown and obsidian edging into them, they were also brimming with sadness, unlike the rest of the deliriously joyful Garrett clan.

The third thing was his scent. Or perhaps it was discovering how much she *liked* it. He smelled, no matter the season, like the sea. Sun-kissed and salty. Not a trace of city grime. And last night, in her office, he'd smelled like the evergreens wrapped around every lamppost in town. As if he'd worn a wreath around his neck. She had worked very hard to contain the urge to press her lips to his glistening skin and take a soulful breath.

When she, with the exception of their brief kiss, had never done something so forward in her life.

Savannah clapped her hands and Macy startled, slipping on the cool facade she used when caught daydreaming and having completely lost her place. She was tucked in one of those darkened corners, content to be passively present. Elle sat beside Savannah on the settee, taking diligent notes, her hand cradling her stomach. She and Noah were expecting a baby in the spring, and she fairly glowed. Savannah and Zach had added to their brood last spring, so the Garrett family was growing in fast measure.

At least this provided business for Macy's

obstetrics practice which, unsurprisingly, was her busiest. No one disagreed with having a female doctor for anything connected to birthing.

If Macy told Caleb no man had made her lose her place during a lecture, that he was the only one she'd experienced a connection with since the incident with her uncle, the only one, possibly, she had ever *desired*, he may not be so vexed about the kiss. When she'd simply wanted to turn him inside out as he did to her without trying. A brief, shared glance across a crowded street enough to make her burst into flames. Again, as she'd stated, the kiss had been a perilous impulse. An undeniable impulse, as it were.

Everyone knew following those was the path to disaster.

Though he'd said he was not angry. Was not *sorry*.

And the opposite of sorry was glad.

The possibility of Caleb Garrett being glad about her popping up on her toes in the dank cloakroom of an assembly hall and pressing her lips, her entire body, to his, made her want to step outside skin suddenly too tight. Of course, the kiss hadn't been exceptional. Because she was new to it. Too, she'd done little research into the process. However...

His eyes *had* gotten a dazed look once or twice last night, so perhaps he'd appreciated her sincere but artless effort. She tapped the pencil on the desk. Maybe, just maybe, he wanted to press his lips to her skin and take a soulful breath, too.

She watched Savannah gesture to Elle as they entered into a passionate discussion and wondered what they would do if she said: *I fear I've developed an attraction for your brother-in-law.*

Yes, Caleb-of-recent-heartbreak. That's the one.

The one who was kind and intelligent and capable, more so than he wanted anyone to know. The one with the dimple that darted his entire cheek when he smiled. The one with work-roughened palms he'd used to capture her hips and pull her against him in the darkness.

The most passionate, searing moment of her life.

He had the long fingers of a pianist, a sculptor, and she wanted them all over her.

Macy ducked her head as a fire lit in her belly and crawled lower, settling in the awakening area between her thighs.

What was happening to her?

Forcing aside musings too captivating to envision in a crowded parlor, she turned her attention to the leaflet, making notes in the column, striking through words, adding context. She loved editing almost as much as she loved performing surgery. Both were important work. Savannah had been quite a force in the suffrage movement in her native New York, and much to the dismay of some, when she married Zach, she decided to continue her efforts from Pilot Isle. She had recruited Macy to assist with advocacy campaigns championing the many medical issues surrounding women and children. Most of the topics were controversial, consequently, the league's members were labeled rabble-rousers and given a wide berth. If there was any bright spot, it was Savannah being married to Pilot Isle's constable. He seemed remarkably skilled at balancing her campaigns against the town's tolerance.

"Is Caleb bringing someone to the tree trimming? The ladies are keeping their distance, even if an available man under the age of eighty is as rare as snow. His perpetual glower is scaring them off."

Macy caught her breath and glanced up to find Savannah circling the room, collecting teacups and wrinkled napkins while Elle stood before a blackboard propped against the wall, erasing a list Macy hoped was inconsequential as she'd not read a word. "Suffering cats, I'm not asking again! You do it this time," Elle said and dusted her hands on her skirt, leaving a streak of white on the dark wool. "*Juste Ciel.* You think Noah is stubborn? Try the middle child if you want to understand how little the Garrett men communicate. He said he's had enough sweetheart-this and darling-that in the past year with all the blasted love in the family and could I please keep my infernal snooping to myself."

Macy bit back a smile.

Savannah laughed and settled the teacups on the sideboard with a clatter. "I simply adore that man."

Elle huffed and gave the blackboard another swipe.

"What fun you must have had growing up. You

and Caleb, why, your escapades are renowned. The revival tent collapsing, the fire in the church. What's the other one? Something about"— Savannah pursed her lips and tapped a teacup against them—"a sinking skiff and the town sending out a search party. I can almost see it. Zach concerned, Noah frantic, Caleb amused. Honestly, he has the best sense of humor of the lot of them. So at odds with his attitude of late."

Elle snapped a length of chalk in half, then frowned at the pieces in her hand. "The old biddies in this town have nothing else to do except chatter, do they? The tent was Cale's fault. The skiff, too. I was the only one who'd sail on his new boats. Can you imagine Noah leaving shore in a craft of uncertain design? I love him more than life itself"—she laid a protective hand over her stomach and the baby growing there—"but a risk-taker, he's not." She tossed the chalk in the tray, her scowl digging deep. "I only stuck my nose in, snooping as Cale termed it, because Noah is worried."

"What about the fire in the church?" At Elle's blank look, Savannah continued, "Caleb's fault, too?"

Elle's lips curled as she ducked her head. "No, that was all me. But Noah, as usual, saved the day. My hero."

"Lucky for us the Garrett brothers are such excellent judges of character."

Elle nodded to Savannah's four-month-old daughter, Regina, sleeping soundly in a bassinette situated in the warmest corner of the parlor. "Zach most of all, it seems."

Savannah propped her elbow on the sideboard and dropped her chin to her fist. "If we figured out what to do about Caleb, life would be close to perfect. And getting the vote in all the states, not only the four out west, would help tremendously, too."

Being around two women reveling in newfound adoration was utterly disheartening when you were so far removed from it. Macy was beginning to see why Caleb's mood had decomposed like a fish stranded on the shore if this is what he had to endure every day. Although hearing about him as a boy was fascinating.

Her childhood—no siblings and aloof parents— had been dismal and forlorn. Macy shifted as her heart gave a squeeze and tapped her pencil against the desk.

"Oh," Savannah murmured, her eyes rounding as she came to a full stand. Elle popped her hand over her mouth, sending a chalky streak across one cheek.

They'd forgotten she was there.

They hadn't called Macy *Mouse* in medical school for nothing. Small, insignificant, and easily overlooked. "Don't worry, ladies. I'm not going to repeat a familial conversation. I—" She halted. I, *what?* I understand Caleb Garrett of the solemn eyes and captivating hands. A little. And maybe you—and this town—have it all wrong. Have him all wrong. Wouldn't *that* be interesting? "I wasn't even really listening." She waved the leaflet in the air, proof of diligent industriousness.

Elle ironed her palm down the front of her skirt and circled her hand in a loopy gesture. "You see, we've tried…" Another hand loop accompanied the partial explanation. "More than once. With Caleb. Advice. Suggestions." She brushed at the chalk on her skirt. "Not receptive."

"Private." Savannah dipped her pinky in a teacup and executed a sluggish stir.

"Stubborn."

"Inflexible."

Elle sighed. "Pigheaded."

Macy smothered a smile while imagining their *advice* and *suggestions*. "Recovery from heartbreak"—which she wasn't entirely certain he was experiencing after his comments and the split-second fiery look in his eyes when she thought, *maybe he'll kiss* me *this time*—"certainly takes time. Like any wound." Like the one she'd stitched the previous evening. Oh, the tantalizing scent of his skin still danced through her mind if she let it. Fantasizing about how delightful a patient smelled had never happened before.

Not once. Not ever.

In fact, until meeting Caleb Garrett, she'd been a veritable model of decorous behavior.

Elle chewed on her lip, her resolute expression quite fearsome. "You could talk to him."

Macy slid back in the chair until her bottom bumped the posts. "Me?"

Elle shrugged as if her suggestion made perfect

sense. "Nudge him along. You're a doctor. Recovery is your game."

"Of the body, not the mind," Macy heard herself say.

Savannah propped her elbow back on the sideboard and slipped into the first slouch Macy had ever seen of her. "Can it be that different? Someone impartial to talk to can be curative. The Hippocratic Oath must include this type of treatment in its text."

"Neutral. Not family," Elle added.

Savannah sucked tea off her pinky. "*Definitely* no family. He's sick of us."

Macy clenched her hands around the seat of the chair. "Why, I—"

"It's quite perfect," Savannah agreed and dipped her finger in the teacup for another go. "And even if it isn't, we're desperate. The boys are starting to bicker beyond what we can stand. Last week, they destroyed my favorite bookcase roughhousing over something Noah said to Caleb that he didn't like. And right now, he doesn't like much."

No, no it wasn't perfect. Not perfect at all.

She was building a sizable crush on the man as swiftly as he was building boats.

Macy wondered if she had the startled look on her face she'd seen on the faces of others who tried to oppose these two. No wonder most in town turned and ran the other way when they saw them coming. "I barely know him. You comprehend this trivial but significant detail, right?"

"A good thing, that. Nothing charming about

the most charming of the Garretts at the moment."
Elle took a last, erasing rub at whatever wisdom
had been on the blackboard. "Tree trimming. My
house, Tuesday. He'll sneak off to the shed out
back like he's always doing lately, and you can
catch him there."

Heavens, catch him and do *what*?

"You said you'd help. In any way," Savannah
reminded her with a none-too-subtle head tilt,
her pinky knuckle-deep in tea.

Macy released the leaflet in defeat. "I meant the
women's league, as you well know." She laughed
and pinched the bridge of her nose to ward off an
impending headache. "Naturally, I will speak to
him. To preserve the sanctity of the Hippocratic
Oath. Although I have one question before I
encroach on his private life. Am I allowed to
tell Caleb my intervention was requested by his
interfering sisters-in-law?"

Elle knocked the eraser against her palm and
coughed as dust rose around her. "Do that, and it's
a complete bust."

Savannah frowned. "He won't listen to a word
you say if he knows we sent you. Stubborn as the
devil when he sets his mind to something."

Macy put the pencil to her lips and recalled the
enticing little dimple that pinged Caleb's cheek
when he smiled. How difficult a challenge, she
wondered, to get him to set his oh-so determined
mind to *her*?

CHAPTER THREE

STANDING IN THE MIDDLE OF a forest searching for the perfect tree was a reasonably mind-numbing activity for a man who didn't really *like* Christmas.

Caleb had never told anyone because it wasn't a sentiment you voiced. *I loathe Christmas.* Comparisons to Dickens's Scrooge and all that. Also, the reason behind his abhorrence would break Zach's heart if he *did* voice it. And this time was a busy one for the Garretts; Zach was the benevolent town constable and someone in the family had to represent at holiday functions. Or so his brother reckoned. So, Caleb plastered on a smile and ate Nora Dorson's sugar cookies even though they tasted like bilge sludge and smelled a bit like vinegar. He danced with women old enough to be his grandmother at Lilian Quinn's musicale, her minuscule parlor feeling like Zach's lone jail cell by the end of the evening. He sat through Reverend Tiernan's midnight service, where napping was impossible because his brother made them sit *on the front row.* He sang carols and wrapped presents and helped tack garlands to posts while striking through the days on his calendar.

Caleb shoved his hands in his coat pockets and

rocked back on his heels. This one, he decided, gazing at the towering fir. Or maybe it was a pine. He tilted his head, debating. An evergreen of some sort. Maybe a cypress. This is what love did to a man, he figured and released a groan that fogged the air around him. Had him in a forest, arguing with himself about a damn tree.

But he did love them. Zach and Noah, little Rory and Regina, Savannah and Elle. To his core. So, he'd find the best tree in Pilot Isle if it would make them happy. One sturdy enough to hold Elle's homemade doodads. Savannah's expensive ornaments from New York. His mother's tattered garland that should have hit the rubbish bin years ago, but no one could bear to part with.

The dank place inside him that grew to immense proportions when the air began to smell like cinnamon and peppermint was *his* problem. He need not tell Noah, and especially Zach, why Christmas caused a dart of unhappiness to center deep in his belly. In his heart. Zach had been piloting when it happened and any mention of turbulence at home while he'd been gone set off the guilt alarms.

Noah, thank God, had been too young to remember.

Christmas should have been a wonderful time when he was a kid. Full of candy sticks and wooden trains, magic only a child can take in and hold. He'd seen how wonderful Zach, and now Savannah, were making it for Rory. And soon, when she was old enough, Regina.

Instead, his father had made it a nightmare.

"This one, huh?" Noah halted beside him, ax slung over his shoulder like he knew what to do with it. A marine biologist and the town's resident genius, he hadn't had many opportunities to split wood, Caleb guessed. "Fraser fir. Excellent choice. I researched the best to go with before we headed out."

"Of course you did," Caleb said with a sigh. A breeze ripped through the trees, sending his coattail flying and the scent of the ocean into his nostrils. Thank God for something reassuring out here.

"The limbs tip, which helps hold ornaments. Excellent needle retention, too, so it'll last until the new year. Similar to a balsam, but I believe this one is a fir. The pyramid shape is unique. Although some scientists suggest the two were once a single species, so you can see the confusion." Noah lowered the ax to his side, and Caleb sidestepped just in case. His brother tended to swing like a man who was trying it out for the first time, every time. "Isn't that fascinating?"

Caleb glanced at him out of the corner of his eye. "Not in the slightest."

Noah picked a piece of bark off the trunk and sniffed. "Definitely a fir."

Zach caught up to them, hat askew, coat partially buttoned, jaw shadowed and in need of a shave. His breath was leaving his mouth in misty puffs. "This it?"

Caleb tugged off his glove with his teeth and

grabbed the ax from Noah. He knew who was getting *this* job. "Reckon so."

"Perfect," Zach said and moved to the closest tree they weren't set on cutting down, propped his back against it, slid to the ground and closed his eyes. Tugging his hat over his face, he slipped into what looked like deep and immediate slumber.

Caleb thrust the ax in his direction. "*Really*? This was his idea!"

"Newborn baby." Noah flipped the bark between his hands, shrugged. "Regina eats every three hours. And the penalty for marrying a reformer, the husband has to share the workload. He's even changing nappies."

"Better get used to zero sleep and lots of poop yourself, Professor. Your little reformer is about to spit one out, too."

Noah skipped the bark over the stalks of chalky, winter-white grass like he would a stone across a lake. "That's passably vulgar, even for you. And you know I hate that nickname." Although a broad smile took hold of his face. Any mention of the baby sent him into joyous spasms.

Caleb ran his fingertip along the blade, determined it would do just fine, and took a test swing. "While you're classifying saplings and Zach catches up on sleep, how about I chop down a Christmas tree so beautiful it will make your wife weep." Holding the ax between his knees, he jerked his glove back on.

"Elle's more of a shouter"—Noah laughed and dodged the kick Caleb sent in his direction—

"but okay. Actually, nothing like pregnancy and a Fraser fir to bring on a nice crying jag. So, go to it."

The first swing felt wonderful, the blade digging in and holding. The raw scent of sap circled, mixing with the aroma of woodsmoke drifting in from town. The pungent sting of the marsh on a rising king tide. Caleb remembered the crude pleasure of demolition. Metal, wood, dominance. It was a basic impulse, to destroy, and basic pleasure derived from it. True, all, but still he experienced the rush. He'd cut down many trees in the days before he had the funds to purchase lumber for his boats. Now, his business was doing so well, he could afford the finest and plenty of it. Could afford that hulking house overlooking the sea. His new warehouse, in a prime location right on the wharf. *Four* part-time employees and maybe more to come by spring. Some days, the success he'd had doing nothing but what he loved, and what he was damned *good* at, made his mind spin.

Reminiscing made him disregard one critical issue. An issue that had the second swing hurting like a bitch. With the pain came an image of Macy's lip caught between her teeth as she stitched him up.

"Ah, shit," he said and let the ax drop to the ground as blood trickled down his arm, soaking the sleeve of his shirt. Beneath layers, he could feel it gumming everything up. "Forgot about that," he grimaced and shrugged out of his coat.

Noah was there before he drew another breath,

mama bear when there'd been no mama since Caleb was twelve years old. "What happened?" His gaze landed on the rosy-red circle blooming on Caleb's sleeve, then bounced until he caught his brother's gaze. "Jesus, Cale," he said even as he was reaching. "You could have said something, you know!"

"Like you can cut down a damn tree." He exhaled and stepped out of his brother's grasp. Son of a bitch throbbed, but he wasn't going to let Noah know that. He'd had enough coddling to last a lifetime. "I'd like to see…the shrub matching your strength."

He'd not only forgotten about the stitches, but the brother sound asleep behind him. Zach stepped into the fray, lifted Caleb's arm in his economical manner, turned it this way and that. "How many? Looks like you've popped most of them, in any case."

"Ten. Maybe twelve." He shook off the hold and pressed his arm to his side. "I don't know. I lost count." Lost count staring into a pair of aquamarine eyes. Like the sea at its highest, deepest, darkest tide. He wanted to bathe in that gaze, go under and never come up for air.

Senseless, but he suspected he was barely concealing a possible, very slight but *probable*, fascination with the lady doctor.

Noah's gaze tracked the blood as it trailed from Caleb's wrist to the tip of his index finger, his jaw flexing like it did when he was trying to contain his ire. "What stitches?" he asked and yanked a handkerchief from his coat pocket and thrust it at Caleb.

Caleb took the cloth and pressed it over the wound. "A minor accident at the warehouse. Nothing to tell. I'm a grown man, unless you've forgotten. You"—he stabbed his finger against Zach's chest, the bloody handkerchief flapping— "have two children to worry about. A wife who runs roughshod over you *and* the town you're busy managing. And you"—he pointed at Noah because jabbing might lead to scuffling, which it often did with this brother, and then where would they be—"have a baby on the way and a wife almost as troublesome. So, can the two of you, please, I'm begging, leave me be?"

"I don't know why you didn't mention an injury when we suggested this. That I may worry about my brother, ridiculous, right?" Zach grabbed the ax and stalked through the woods, his hat blowing off his head and fluttering to the ground. "Leland's going to slam the door in our faces when we ask him to repair the stitches. After each one of us has knocked him on his ass in the past few months, I guess I don't blame him." Zach tracked back, grabbed his hat and stuffed it on his head. Pine straw clung to it and shot out at all angles. "Well, boyo, you can bet a shiny new nickel that scar is going to be purposely hideous."

Caleb waited until they'd started walking again, dodging trees, before he corrected the error. "Miss Dallas did the stitching."

The unconcealed shock on their faces tasted

better than a shot of whiskey. Better than a slice of Elle's glorious red velvet cake. "I wouldn't go to Leland for a hangnail," he added, trying to hold back his grin. Damn, if this wasn't starting to amuse. And after months of listening to these lovesick fools, he deserved any delight he could get.

"Elle made you do it," Noah whispered with a look of horror.

Zach grunted, kicking a limb stretched across their path. "A dozen new streetlamps didn't satisfy. Repaired sidewalks, check. More feminine products at the mercantile. Another check. Now they want the vote. Equal employment at Noah's lab. Why not flood the town with women doctors? Hell, I guess I'll go to her since Leland is out."

"She's smart." Caleb tugged his cap over his ears. Without his coat, the wintry bite was starting to sting. "Capable." He blew into his cupped fist and hunched his shoulders, his wound violently protesting the movement. "Neatest row of stitches you've ever seen. Leland's a butcher in comparison. And I have the scars to prove it."

Noah sidestepped a fallen log, his gaze sliding Caleb's way. He was the clever one, the handsome one. While Zach was the honorable one, the protector. That left Caleb to be the Garrett who messed things up, went in temper thundering, brain nowhere in sight. He didn't know quite how to define himself.

He simply knew he was not the *good* brother.

Feeling the heat of Noah's stare, he returned it

until his brother dropped his gaze. Caleb recorded the wheels spinning as the Professor tried to figure out how to ask what he wanted to ask. "Your decision to go to her, then?" was what he came up with.

Caleb quit the pine thicket and halted by the wagon they'd left parked on the road leading to the mainland ferry. It was new, built by the finest manufacturer in North Carolina, able to haul any amount of lumber he chose to place in it. Saying he was pleased with the vehicle would be an understatement. He draped his coat over his shoulders as he hoisted himself into the high-backed seat. The sun was setting, the cold really digging in, and his wound thumping unmercifully. "Who else's would it be?"

Noah climbed in beside him and propped his booted feet atop the toe board. "Am I not allowed to be surprised?"

"Don't start," Caleb growled and looped the reins around his fist. His horse danced in place, and he gentled her with a murmur. "I can tell you're going to start something. You have that interfering look."

"Savannah's going to kill me, coming home empty-handed," Zach muttered as he climbed into the wagon bed. "Now I'll have to buy one of Flint Newsome's pitiful pines. They start shedding the day you bring them home. Dead by Christmas. I thought..." He rocked back against the plank wall with a sigh. "Never mind."

Caleb half-turned on the seat. "You thought

what exactly?"

"Well, since you're asking in the charming tone you use of late, I'll admit I hoped we might push you back into the light, into living. Everyone loves the holidays. A festive activity to get you out of that warehouse, your mausoleum on the cliff. I know Christabel broke your—"

"Enough," Caleb said through clenched teeth as he drew back on the reins, sending his horse into a sidestepping canter. "I'm *not* heartbroken, that's just it. I'm empty"—he bumped the heel of his hand on his stomach—"because losing her didn't hurt as badly as it should have. As I thought it would. Because she was right." *I'm not for you in the way you imagine, Caleb. The way you want us to be. Like Noah and Elle, Zach and Savannah. Can't you see the difference? It's whispers in the dark. Looks across a crowded room. The less* and *the more.*

The less and the more.

He wasn't sure what Christabel meant by that, but he wanted to find out.

Macy's tender, inexperienced kiss had unlocked something inside him. Woken him from a dreadfully secluded slumber. Opened his mind, if not his heart, to a dazzling promise.

The scary thing was, he wanted more than a quick dip in those sapphire eyes. Sex, he'd manage just fine and come out alive, but this was *more.* He wanted to fix her run-down house. Build her a lovely skiff with butter-yellow sails, one he'd spot the moment he saw it gliding over the waves. Compel the townspeople to believe in her medical skills like he did.

They weren't all noble, his wants. He was a man, through and through. In his big, lonely bed, he stroked himself and dreamed of her in every position he could come up with and then some. His cock twitched in his breeches as if to say, *yes, you have.* She'd become a fixation, acute need throbbing just beneath his skin.

He wanted, and he wanted *desperately.*

With a click of his tongue and a yank on the reins, he put the wagon into motion. This was too much deep thought for a man who didn't think deeply. At least his unexpected speech had stunned his brothers into silence. He prayed for a peaceful ride into town. No more talk of empty houses and women disappearing from your life when you least expected it. No more wishing you were good enough for someone when you knew you weren't.

He could tell them…

He could tell them…

He believed in love. And he wasn't scared of loving someone.

He was scared of falling in love and of her not falling in love back.

CHAPTER FOUR

MACY STEPPED THROUGH THE DOOR of Caleb's warehouse and into another world.

Sunlight from narrow windows set just below the beamed ceiling pierced the air at hard angles to gather in pools on the heart pine floor. The smell of glue and raw wood, linseed oil and a masculine undertone she guessed must be his, swept over her.

As did the music.

She turned a full circle, searching for the source. Joplin, if she was not mistaken. And she wasn't. Music was her second love next to medicine. Other than those, she'd never had anything, or anyone, to be passionate about.

Perhaps it was time to change that. To leave the Mouse behind.

She followed the rasping sound until she found him, leaning over the bow of a partially completed skiff, his hands a gentle glide over gleaming wood. He was dressed for labor in an open-collar shirt and work breeches that hugged his muscular body the way the sea did the shore. He shouldered a bead of sweat from his brow, stepped back to eye his work, then moved in and set the plane to wood. Hair the color of the sky at midnight tumbled over his brow, and she had to stop herself from brushing it back. She yearned to tangle her fingers in the tousled strands, see for herself if it felt as soft as it looked.

What a fine specimen he was. Certainly, better than any drawing from anatomy class. He was real, and her base desire was to *explore*. As she studied him, a spiral lit and spread through her, the sensation dancing along her arms, down her thighs and out the soles of her feet, rocking her where she stood.

So, this is what unbridled desire feels like.

"What took you so long?" Caleb asked without looking up, his hand smoothing over the spot he'd set the plane to as if he searched for another imperfection. "Couldn't have taken Noah more than ten minutes after I dropped him off to get to you."

She placed her medical bag on a rough-hewn table shoved against the wall, moving aside incongruent items: hammer, book, comb. "Noah came by, yes. Said you were too stubborn to come to my office yourself. Actually, your sisters—in-law, that is—brought me here. Requested my presence, rather. 'Forced' could be stated without duplicity."

He swiped his hair out of his eyes. Oh, they were lovely in this sunlight. "*Really.*"

"Very persuasive. Frightening, actually." She rotated the book. *The Picture of Dorian Gray.* Interesting. "They wanted me to talk to you. A therapeutic session, if I understood correctly.

Because you've been destroying furniture." She smiled softly, trying to get him to take the bait and smile back. "I promised I wouldn't tell. But here I am, doing just that."

He placed the plane on the bow, stood to his full height, and stretched with a low groan that slipped beneath her skin like a splinter. Her mouth watered as he twisted, flexed, shifted on the balls of his feet. Such graceful movements for a large man. No way to deny it, she was dazzled.

"So, you're breaking a promise."

She brought herself back to the conversation, found him watching her watch him. Heat hit her cheeks, a blast of embarrassment. The payoff was the subtlest hint of amusement curving his lips. Her discomfiture entertained.

His smile was worth any discomfort, she decided.

"Yes." She opened her medical bag and began to arrange the items she needed to repair his torn stitches, stacked gauze, needle, and thread right beside the ever-charming *Dorian Gray*. "But I'm keeping one to you."

He held her gaze until the workroom began to feel like a greenhouse even with a stalwart breeze rolling off the sea and through the open stable doors. What they were cultivating inside this fascinating space, she didn't know. Yet the spiral of excitement, no, *wonder*, overtaking her mind and body felt like magic. A miracle after being alone for so long, fearing she'd never find her way out of the darkness. For being shaken from sleep after dozing for years.

To escape the penetrating silence and the intensity of his gaze, she lifted hers, noticing for the first time the charcoal sketches tacked on the wall behind him. They were luminous. Detailed, stunning. She'd seen poorer examples in a gallery. "These are yours?"

He tossed a quick look over his shoulder. "Have to draw what you build. At least I do."

"You're an artist," she breathed and stepped in to review one up close. Trailed her fingertip over the remarkably rendered illustration, so vivid she could almost hear waves slapping the hull, taste a salty grit on her tongue. Her father had had a small sailing vessel, she wasn't even sure what kind, and she'd stood on the shore of the lake behind their home, observing as he sailed off without her. Time and time again. He hadn't wanted companionship. Or a daughter. So, she'd struggled to fill the void. Every decision, including those appalling ones involving her uncle, had derived from trying to plug the hollow space inside her.

To please a man no one could please.

Behind her, Caleb fidgeted, his boots a faint scuffle on pine planks. His unease provided a tantalizing peek into the soul buried beneath slightly wrinkled clothing and a scowl that was weak around the edges if you looked closely. Incredibly, she had never met a man who secreted his accomplishments, his strength, his intelligence, in the way this one did. He was so much more than he believed and, somehow, *he had no idea.* She'd been in Pilot Isle long enough to appreciate the delicacy of his position. Stuck solidly between two brothers: one a prodigy, the other the magnanimous town leader. They'd had their places carved out for longer than anyone could remember.

Where did that leave Caleb?

She remembered what it was like to be lost amidst family. Where one should feel the most comfort and security…but simply didn't. Hers had been ripped away. But there had been no one around to protect her.

"The drawing you're studying like you have an exam coming up is a cutter. It'd be my biggest build, if—how would Noah say it—the project comes to fruition." His arm brushed her shoulder as he reached, a whisper-light touch that made her breath catch. Caleb tapped the sketch in two places, and Macy tracked the movement like she'd stitched her gaze to his finger. "Double-masted, gaff-rigged. Designed for speed rather than capacity. Two headsails and a long bowsprit. It's quite…" He stepped back, taking the warmth engulfing her with him. "It's a magnificent design, if I do say so myself."

Tilting her head, she found him studying her like *he* had an exam. "I don't have any idea what that means," she said, laughing softly.

"It means it's going to rip like hell across the waves and look gorgeous doing it," he returned as his eyes politely but openly devoured her. Steady regard unlike any she'd experienced in her life.

Steady enough to have her knees shaking beneath copious, ridiculous layers. To send an ache between her legs she was sure she'd answer the call for in her bedroom this very evening.

"I'm not good on the water, which I know is odd when I live on the coast. I'm not even a strong swimmer. I didn't grow up, that is my parents—" She halted, gestured inanely.

"I'll need to test this one in a week or so." He jacked his thumb over his shoulder, indicating the boat he'd been working on. "I could take you sailing. The next calm day. It's not hard to find your sea legs." His gaze did a slow roll to her feet and heat blew through her. "I guarantee they're there somewhere."

She directed her attention back to his sketch, imagined his fingers gripping the charcoal pencil. Sliding over her skin. Knotting in her hair. Dipping beneath her drawers and touching her as she'd touched herself while thinking about him. *Sea legs, indeed.* "I heard about your experiments with Elle," she said with a voice gone as dry as the sawdust beneath their feet. "She ended up in the ocean."

He made no reply, allowing the silence to settle around them. He was a patient man, unhurried and not absorbed with hurrying *her*. She liked it. His earnestness, his willingness to cede control when men usually felt they had to command the room, *any* room, made her feel...safe.

Imagine that? *Safe.*

"I'd never let anything happen to you," he

murmured. "Elle was a remarkably strong swimmer. A quick dunk wasn't going to hurt her."

She turned to find him stuck to the same spot, not having moved a muscle, his head tipped toward the floor. "I know. Somehow, even though we're newly acquainted"—she pressed her hand to her belly, where a pulse thumped beneath her palm because her mind had started replaying their kiss—"I know."

Heavens if she didn't lose every thought in her head when he lifted his and a *genuine* smile, full and beautiful, sat on his face, sending that recalcitrant dimple flaring to life. *Ah, there's the charming man I've heard about.* Sly whispers across a crowded tea table at the women's league meeting, over the clack and thrust of knitting needles at the sewing circle. The women in town had prepared her in a way: quick to laugh, always the first to volunteer, so in love with his family. She'd known *that* Caleb Garrett was in there somewhere.

Never one to ignore an opportunity, she seized on his delight and gestured to the lone stool in the room. Tapped her shoulder, indicating his. "May I?"

He gave her one of those easy laughs but with no explanation behind it. "Sure, Doc, do your worst."

"I'll do my best."

"Your best works, too." Her breath caught as he unbuttoned his shirt, tugged down the sleeve covering his injured arm, keeping the other hanging from his shoulder like a sheet partially concealing a sculpture. He perched on the wobbly stool, material fluttering around his hips. With partial success, she kept her gaze from tracking the dusting of dark hair trailing between his pectorals in a straight shot to his groin. She cleaned the wound and assessed damage to her earlier repair, forcing her mind to medicine. *Pectoralis major. Assists in creating lateral, vertical, or rotational motion. Pectoralis minor...*

He sat through her ministrations with nothing more than one sharp intake of air that sent his lashes fluttering and her stomach sinking to her knees. *No man should have lashes so long*, she reasoned in mild disgust.

"Why the grunt of displeasure? The popped stitches? It was my fool brother's fault, I'm telling you." He palmed the wall to hold the stool steady. "I'd share the story, but it's a painful retelling."

"Ladies do not grunt," she informed him as she went through the steps of applying a clean dressing. *So, he wanted to know, did he?* She decided, right then and there, to tell him. "My modest token of protest was because you have the longest lashes I've ever seen on a man, and as a woman who has somewhat stubby ones herself, I find this terribly unfair."

A crinkle formed between his brows as his hand left the wall, before he caught himself and dropped his curled fist to his lap. "That's ridiculous."

"Ridiculous for a man to have such long lashes, I agree," she replied as she bound his arm with a bandage she hoped he protected this time. As she finished tying off the length of gauze—and she could not say exactly why she did it, perhaps it was because he smelled of spice and sunlight and she wanted to bathe in the scent—she trailed her index finger down his forearm to his wrist. Then she stared at him as she kept it there, over his pulse, which skipped and fired into a swift beat.

She knew her actions were unseemly. Knew she should not want to touch him, *know* him, inside and out, in the powerful way she did. Knew he likely found *her* ridiculous. Too serious. Quiet. Uninteresting.

The things she'd always been.

But she also knew she'd never felt this way about a man—and her heart had sealed itself off thinking she never would. So, she took it a step further and circled his wrist, confirming her request. Because she had a feeling, a very definite one, that he was too much a gentleman to do so himself.

"Why me?" he asked as his blood danced beneath her fingertips. "When you could have any man in this town? In any town?"

A tremor shook her; they were leaving the dock and entering deep water. No going back now. The music paused as the wax cylinder in his phonograph skipped, then Joplin glided back over them like a tepid breath. *If you only understood how your kiss revived me.* "I…" She swallowed and stepped back, into the table. *Dorian Gray* hit the floor with a thump. Nonplussed, she went to her knees to pick it up, and he followed.

As they crouched in the muted sunlight, he

slipped his knuckle beneath her chin, tipping her head until her gaze met his. "I'm not a caretaker, Macy Dallas. That's why I'm alone. Zach's the Garrett for that job. Or Noah. I'm the brother who goes off half-cocked. A bull set loose in the china shop. Destructive and thoughtless. I know how to build boats, but I don't know how to build what you need. I never have."

"I don't believe—"

"*Doc.*" He swept his thumb along her jaw, tucking a strand of hair behind her ear. "I'm not the one, whatever, whoever, it is you're looking for. But I find myself fantasizing about you so often of late, I'm almost willing to volunteer. Waking in the darkest pitch of night reaching for you, remembering the feel of your lips beneath mine. Even if I'm no good for you. Even if it's mostly me who's going to benefit"—he traced the shell of her ear—"I still find myself wanting you. I can't seem to help myself."

She licked her lips, her heartbeat spiking as his pupils flooded pewter. "Mrs. Schumacher said you were always the first to volunteer."

He sighed, sending those long lashes fluttering. "The way you stare at me doesn't help."

How did *she stare at him?*

He leaned in, his hand sliding to cradle her neck. Into her hair, his fingertips were rough against her scalp, his breath cinnamon-scented and scalding her cheek. "You look at me like I'm gonna hang the moon. Or make your dreams come true. When I'm not, I'm telling you. And this…" The hand caressing the nape of her neck tightened as he gripped her waist with the other and inched her forward, trapping her knees inside his own.

She swayed, flattening her hands on his chest to steady herself. He was so close, too close, and it felt *wonderful*.

"If you said it was just kisses you want, I wouldn't trust you. I could say the same and, hell, I wouldn't trust myself. I could tell you I kissed you back in that cloakroom because I was lost from the moment you touched me. Blind with desire for you, mad with it. That it's only deepened every time I watch you cross a crowded street, looking through fripperies in the mercantile. Painting those women's rights signs with Savannah and Elle. That I lay in bed each night hungering for you, for *us*. I don't like building anything without a plan telling me exactly what I'm building. And you, this…" His fingers worked deeper into her hair, sending pins to the floor as her chignon collapsed atop his fist. "I don't know what this is. What I'm feeling." He laid his lips to her brow, her cheek and drew a breath as if he wanted to take her into his lungs like oxygen. "But it's impressive."

"Is it her?" she asked as she noted the crescent scar running alongside his nose, the freckle on his chin she wanted to press her mouth against. It made her feel possessive to be close enough to gather these intimate things about him. Her own personal box of Caleb Garrett treasures. If he let her, she would draw a map noting each point of interest on his body. Drawn with her lips, her tongue, her teeth. "Are you truly so heartbroken?"

He bent his broad body until they were eye-level, like it was urgent she understand what he was about to say. His eyes had gone gunmetal and were shimmering in the fading sunlight. Stubble dotted his jaw, giving him a sinister look when he was far from fearsome. "I'm *not* and neither is she. Don't you see? That's the confounding, sad truth of it. It's not that I've been stung, like all the biddies are saying, and now I'm giving females a wide path 'til I forget how much the venom hurt. I'm…" He rocked back on his heels but kept his hold on her. His gaze on her. "I'm afraid of heartbreak with the *right* woman, not heartbreak over losing the wrong one."

Her heart expanded in her chest, bumping against her ribs. "You're afraid of *love*?"

Still kneeling, he pulled her to him, their bodies sealing from hip to chest. Each valley of hers perfectly met a peak of his, a most splendid fit. "And spiders."

"Not kisses," she whispered as his lips grazed hers, a fleeting stroke, barely there but for the lingering scent of him clouding the air she breathed. His skin was warm beneath the thin cloth of his shirt, searing her palms, his muscles rippling as he angled their bodies for closer contact.

"Never kisses," he murmured as his lids slipped low. He sucked her bottom lip between his and feasted, gently, thoroughly, causing her legs to tremble. With a sigh, she fell against him. His arm slipped lower, circling her waist, holding her tightly as his mouth left hers to bite, suck, lick. Her skin sizzled with longing at each point he attended. Her throat ached; her nipples hardened until the scrape against muslin was almost painful.

And the area between her thighs—where she touched herself while she imagined touching *him*—awakened and bloomed. "Stop toying… with me," she gasped as he nipped her earlobe, then pressed it between his lips to soothe. Once, twice, a third time.

"Ah, Doc, if I was toying with you"—his breath thundered like the sea as it swept past—"you would know it."

She worked her hand between their bodies as he explored the sensitive area below her jaw, the nape of her neck. Who knew vibrations could flow from head to toe as if sent on a telegraph wire, click, click, click?

If he explored, so would she.

After all, she'd dreamed of this.

Collarbone. *Clavicle. Links Sternum to scapula.* Ribs. *Latin: costae.* Abdomen. *Abdodere.* Stomach. *Ventriculus.* His skin was flushed, moist, velvet-smooth in some areas, rough and scarred in others. Muscle contracted where she touched, heaving with his breath, which had intensified as she'd progressed. When she reached the waistband of his breeches, he exhaled and forcibly moved her away from him.

She blinked, searching for time and place.

Her body submerged, engrossed, liquified. Like beakers over a gas flame, the contents bubbling, ablaze.

He gave her a gentle shake. "I lied. I *am* toying with you."

"This isn't—"

Moving to cup her face, he seized her mouth. Slanted his head for a richer connection, one reaching to her marrow. His participation had been negligible, controlled, before this moment. *Oh, how he'd been toying.* His tongue engaged, invited, parried. She could only follow, duplicate, counter. He rose to his feet, bringing her with him without breaking contact. His hands swept her body, settling on her hips and guiding her back into the table. Then he pressed, leaving her no room to move. Sensation from all sides, all senses. The scent of labor and raw wood, cinnamon and an elementally male essence she couldn't define. The brackish rush of air from an open window. Splintered wood from the table pricking her cotton shirtwaist. Joplin a haunting presence circling the room.

Caleb. Muscular, broad, formidable. Gentle. His hand trembling where he gripped her jaw; his voice ragged, unintelligible murmurs she neither deciphered nor absorbed. Not when those beautiful, artistic fingers were touching her. *Finally.*

She was astounded that he appeared as taken with her as she was with him.

As vanquished. As famished.

The roll of gauze fell to the floor as they bumped the table. His hand clenched, fingertips a hard press into her hip. He sighed and trailed his hand up her body, his fingers delving into her hair and tangling as he extended the kiss. Slowed, drawing on her bottom lip. Teasing bites, his tongue tracing the edges after. Soothing, playful. This touch, this frolic, went with the smile he unveiled earlier, the easy laugh. The side of him he'd hidden from her, from everyone, for so long.

She was trapped inside his arms, contained on all sides, the most sensual hug imaginable.

Forget his brother. *Caleb* was the genius.

She murmured a plea against his lips and shifted, restless. *More.* Her breasts were aching, her thighs throbbing. She'd chosen him, which he did not understand the importance of. To pull her from the darkness. To make her *feel* again. The mechanics were straightforward and ones she understood. Her virtue mattered little. Her heart, if it became engaged, a problem she would deal with.

The joy of this, the true gift: she had faith again.

For the first time, she *trusted* a man. For a person of medicine, it bewildered her how unbelievably healing this felt.

Returning the kiss with equal fervor, she worked his sleeve down his uninjured arm and let his shirt drift to the floor. As her hands caressed, explored, Latin once again swept her mind, a sing-song chant pulsing in time with her heartbeat. *Caro. Cor. Corpus. Coxa.* This rather than visualize his penis, which was a rigid presence against her hip, inviting, calling to her.

She wanted to *consume*.

"Wait," he gasped and released her. "Hold on a second. Hold. On. A. Second."

She grabbed his hand, linked their fingers and yanked him closer. "Oh, no. No. Don't back out now. Not when I, you…" She gestured to the delightful erection tenting his breeches. "*Really*?"

He tugged his free hand through his hair, sending it into splendid disarray. "You must be losing your mind if you think I—" He blew out a hard breath, his eyes a slate glimmer in the dying sunlight. "I'm not saying no. God, do you not know men. I was simply going to tell you, if you're certain, positively sure about this, saying yes, a *clear* yes, I have a bedroom here. I spend a lot of nights working on—"

"*Yes*." She turned a half-circle, taking him and their linked hands with her. "Where's the bed?"

With a growl, he lifted her off her feet and tossed her over his shoulder as if she weighed nothing. The bulge of muscle in his biceps was phenomenally impressive and quite arousing.

She laughed as he stalked through the warehouse and entered a back room, where he unceremoniously dropped her atop a bed large enough to house an entire family. "Watch those stitches," she ordered.

"Yes, ma'am," he whispered and rolled over her like a wave.

Heartbroken, she thought and shook her head in

delight as his lips captured hers.

Pilot Isle was filled with a bunch of fools.

And she the most lovesick of them all.

The throaty sigh Macy released as he settled over her luscious little body about did him in, drowning out the roar of waves hammering the wharf, the faint thread of ragtime spitting from his phonograph. His heartbeat pulsing in his ears.

Perching on his elbows to keep from placing his full weight on her, Caleb paused to gaze at her, not quite believing she was there. But she was, in the monstrosity of a bed he'd ordered from High Point for the simple reason that he liked it, an indulgence he could now afford. Her hair was a flaxen cascade over his drab counterpane, her magical eyes glinting in the sunset glow filtering through the window above them. She was every dream he'd ever had come to life. A mix of traits that charmed and captivated. Intelligent, beautiful, shy.

He'd frequently pictured her in this modest sanctuary tucked inside his somewhat forbidding warehouse. Stroked himself to dazzling completion while imagining her beneath him. Bent over his worktable, laid across the bow of a skiff. Riding him, her legs locked around his as she clutched his body to her own. Touching, licking, *devouring*.

It would take a year to recreate the many ways he'd dreamed of pleasuring Macy Dallas.

Desire struck hard, harder than he remembered

it hitting, washing over him like the sea on a summer day. *She was his.* For an hour, or a night.

And make no mistake: he would take her.

He didn't know why she wanted him. He wasn't nearly good enough. Somehow, they were all wrong. *He* was all wrong.

But he was also weak.

What she offered, he could not refuse. Because she'd made him feel alive again. Wanted. Special. Entirely separate from the Garrett mystique. For once, his own man.

He was infatuated, he admitted, as he cupped her breast, found the nipple straining beneath her thin shirtwaist. Caressed it with his thumb, circle, stroke, repeat, until her back bowed and her lids quivered. Until a raspy moan shot from her throat. Until his cock stiffened to an unbearable degree, making him worry over how long he'd last this first time.

He wouldn't take their relationship further than this evening, not with such a grave risk to his heart. Or hers. Still, he was good at boatbuilding, and truthfully, he was good at *this*. She didn't know it, but lovemaking could be tender and ferocious at the same time. An erotic mix with so many fine options, a different one for each day of the week for a hundred years.

When you trusted who you were with.

She was hiding in a manner he had yet to figure. Like a puppy who'd been kicked, she was fearful. Of men, he suspected. Maybe even of being touched. A streak of raw anger pulsed through him as he pictured why. And maybe he was wrong…but he didn't think so.

So, he'd show her pleasure and pray he wasn't losing his heart in the process.

This was the only promise he could make.

He rolled to his feet, and while she observed through a gaze gone misty, toed his boots off. Unbuttoned his breeches, removed those and his drawers. When he had nothing left to remove, he grasped her ankle and tugged her across his monstrous bed, her legs dropping on either side of him, thighs spread. "Macy Dallas, you're so beautiful it almost hurts to look at you." He nudged her skirt to her knee and drew a wispy loop on her thigh. Her breath kicked, her eyes flooding cobalt. Her scent, a flowery concoction, circled, scattering thought, squeezing him in a tight fist of longing. "I'm going to undress you, then get to know your body so well I could sketch you without you being in the room."

She closed her eyes on the vow as he began to remove layers.

Senseless, how many of them a man had to work through to get to skin, but it was so pleasing to touch a woman's frilly nothings again. And he was patient, if nothing else. Delicate lace, fancy bone buttons, satin ribbons. She made no protest, shifting her body when needed to facilitate the process. Shirtwaist, skirt, corset, petticoats, chemise, drawers. Nearing the end, he propped her heel atop his thigh and worked her stocking down her leg. Brought her foot to his lips and swirled his tongue over her ankle, which sent a flush to her cheeks, crested her nipples to hard peaks and had her breath shattering. His hands shaking now, he repeated with the other leg, kissing her knee, her thigh. Her skin was soft, slightly moist, and tasting of roses. The scent of her core drifted to him, and he knew he wasn't going to last long.

Okay, the first time, inevitably hurried but gentle. Orgasm for each of them to take the edge off—maybe two for her—then they could get to the real business of making love.

Plan in place, he made to climb on the bed, but she propped her foot on his belly, halting him. And giving him a direct view at the flaxen curls between her thighs, an area he hoped to visit with lips, tongue, and teeth before too long. The night had dissolved into silver twilight, and he recorded its glide over her thighs, her tummy, her breasts. Ones, for such a petite sprite, he was overjoyed by the size of. Her lovely face. Those wild eyes. He didn't press, though he wanted to dive inside her more than he wanted his next breath.

His desire could wait. He could wait. He was hers to use this evening in any manner she proposed.

Or not, if it came to that.

The hand he held against the bed trembled and the quiver ricocheted up his arm, her gaze recording it all. Her resulting smile was soft, sweet, guileless if he had to pick a word. One of Noah's words but fitting. And he realized a moment's terror, true fear, because her reaction sent an arrow—or what felt like one—directly at his heart.

With her smile came daring.

Her foot slid down his belly and over his cock, which jutted at a greedy angle. His groan was one he was unable to suppress. "Is this punishment?" he rasped. "For ripping up those stitches?"

"*Come,*" she whispered, low, throaty and final. Her arms rose, beckoning. Like she waited in harbor for him to sail back to shore.

So, he did. Spreading her body back on his colorless bedding when she was all the color in the world. Lighting the room with her brilliance. He settled between her legs as if she'd been made for him, the perfect shelter from his storm of a life. "I'm too heavy for you," he said. *I'm many things wrong for you.*

She wrapped her arms around him and drew him close, pressed her lips to the sensitive spot between neck and shoulder and suckled. His skin plainly caught fire. "You're perfect, Caleb Garrett, simply perfect."

He wasn't, but he would damn-well try to be.

He started with kissing, as they'd already established a rhythm there. And he'd kinda figured out what she liked: deliberate, penetrating contact. Thorough. *Damn,* she tasted good. Like cotton candy, light and wispy but oh, so sweet. He could feast on nothing but her lips for days.

He waited for her signal, the shift of her hips, her wiggle against his cock, which was wedged quite snuggly in her moistening folds. Her legs rising, knees digging into his hips for purchase.

It was his signal to head south.

He threw one last glance at her, outlined in the blue-black twilight, and raised her arms above her head, linking her fingers around his spindled headboard. Her hair was a golden shroud, chest riding her quick breaths. "Hang on, love."

Her breasts were heavy, round as apples, the nipples the exact color of the inside of a conch shell. Pink mixed with hints of amber. At the first touch of his lips, she gasped, tangled a hand in his hair and bowed into the touch. How long since he'd had a woman's nails digging into his skin, her muscles contracting beneath his own? Her nipple hardening beneath his lips. Her moan of pleasure soothing the murky places inside him. He sucked one, then the other, alternating. Teeth, tongue, the rough edge of his palm, which sent her into spasms of delight. Contrast, pressure, release.

When she whimpered, wrapped her hands around those spindles and knocked her pelvis against his, he acknowledged that the clock was ticking on her release. He admired every area he could on the way down. Her gently rounded belly, her hip, the inside of her thigh. His hands were busy, until he guessed she was having a hard time keeping up.

He didn't want her to keep up.

He wanted her to trust him to unlock this box she'd been hiding herself in.

Her sex was glistening, her legs flung wide. She

wasn't shy about her arousal, an unexpectedly gratifying piece of herself she shared. He touched, lightly. Softly. Along her seam and back. Inched his finger inside her to the first knuckle. Then the second when her body let him know he could. She arched and gasped into his touch, drawing him deeper. Pausing, he watched her writhe upon his bed.

She was the most enticing thing he'd ever seen.

Delirious with longing, he tried to buy them both time by running calculations for a single-masted sloop in his head. Her skin was hot, moist, her cries, murmurs, moans, loud enough to bury Joplin. Boy, he'd never be able to hear *that* tune again without embarrassing himself.

He slid another finger inside her, a leisurely glide. Lowered his lips and kissed her. *There.* Circled the nub holding the answer to her release with his tongue. Recorded what she liked, what move made her moan the loudest. She was begging now, and he hadn't the heart to extend the performance, even selfishly.

"More. Yes. Harder, Cale, *harder.*"

He tunneled his arm beneath her and lifted her to his mouth, finished with tender exploration. This was reckless desire, unchanneled. His damn plan splintered like wood beneath a brutal hammer blow. He wanted with a fierce compulsion. To please her, to please himself, to *love.* "Don't hold back," he whispered, his breath skimming her skin. "I'm here."

She clutched his shoulders, tangled her fingers

in his hair, and cried out as she came around him, her back arching. Tightening around his tongue and fingers in blissful torment.

Her release was *his*.

Unmooring him from regret and fear, if only for one moment.

Once she'd steadied, he laid her tenderly on the bed. Smoothed his palm over her body like he was planing wood. She swallowed hard, slight pleasure tremors still rocking her. Her eyes when they met his had tinted black. "This explains… the comments at the sewing circle."

A laugh sputtered from his lips. "*What?*"

"*Please*. As if. You—" She lifted her arm, did a vague finger-flick in his direction, then let it flop to the mattress. "You waged war, right there between my legs."

He sat back on his heels, the mattress dipping. Waged war, had he? Damn if he didn't like the sound of that. "Did I win?"

She jerked the pillow from beneath her head and tossed it at him. A girl's throw that went a mile wide. Her reply broke through her amusement. "Yes, blast you, you won mightily."

"Okay, then," he said and crawled up the bed, determined to wage another, right this very minute.

CHAPTER FIVE

MACY HAD NOT IMAGINED LAUGHTER to be a part of sexual congress.

Likewise, the mechanics, the anatomical piece, which she had a firm grasp on, didn't fit, either. Not quite. Caleb was teaching her things she hadn't expected to learn. Truthfully, lovemaking wasn't at *all* what she'd expected when she followed blind need down a not-so-well-lit garden path.

His playfulness, for one. And his patience. Both challenged her modest expectations. He was sensitive, respectful, *generous*. His body *fit* hers. Caleb's big, incredible body fit hers, she concluded as he lowered his hips into place between her thighs. Also, he'd done unspeakable, amazing things to her with his mouth.

And she'd not only let him, she'd been comfortable doing so. Safe and protected.

Hungry, desirous, wild.

Again, please.

There'd been that moment, when she hadn't decided, with her foot wedged against his belly, whether she wished to claim him or push him away. Then his kindness shone a bright light on her decision. He hadn't pressed. He'd merely waited. For her.

It was a revelation.

A *fun* discovery, when life threw so few of those her way. No woman of her acquaintance had ever, *ever*, told her lovemaking was agreeable. Savannah and Elle had hinted at a positive experience, but everyone else?

Untidy. Painful. *Boring.*

When *it* was fascinating. *He* was fascinating. His radiance bleeding like paint spilled from a can and coloring *her* interesting. He was a creator, a designer, an artist. Elinor Macy Dallas—otherwise known as the Mouse—making a virile man like Caleb pant, tremble and want was beyond her comprehension.

Take that, Johns Hopkins Medical School class of 98'. The Mouse is no more.

Her final thought as he drove his fingers into her hair and shifted her mouth to his was: *how do I keep him?*

Their kisses grew reckless, their touches bold. Inflaming, inciting. They were a damp tangle of arms and legs across the bed and against the headboard. Without giving her a moment's respite, he continued the worship of her body. Teeth scraping her collarbone. Lips caressing her nipples. Fingers stroking inside her. His particular, intensely erotic scent imprisoning her.

Releasing a harsh exhalation, he pulled back, gazed into her eyes and adjusted below, his rigid tip meeting her juncture, a stimulating challenge. "Don't worry, I'll go—"

She cut him off with a kiss, dug her nails into

his back and lifted her hips to bring him home. He rocked into her slowly, as she guessed he'd been about to promise to. There was one brief, painful flare, then only the delightful weight of him, stretching, probing. Setting off sparks inside her. Like sun shimmers across cresting waves, zaps traveling from her lips to her toes. When they were locked as deeply as humanly possible, he began to move, sliding out to the absolute brink, then pausing at the end of the stroke, whispering, seeking approval. Guidance. Divine intervention.

"Amazing," she breathed and locked her legs around his waist. "*You.*"

He groaned low in his throat and clutched her bottom, increasing his speed, his thrusts lifting her off the mattress. He had left behind his measured playfulness and replaced it with resolute purpose. Lost to sensation, she was unable to do more than move with him, groan and gasp with him. Accept his bottomless kisses and let them flow through to her soul. Grasping her thigh, he angled her leg around his hip. Deeper admittance, gentle but devastating.

They were a jumble of moist skin, feverish need, turbulent desire. *Want.* She craved him with a keenness that threatened to break her. Gloriously, he filled every vacant space until they seemed two halves of one body, flawlessly allied.

"I can't...much longer, sweetheart. Too good, too much."

She watched, transfixed, as he surrendered to her. Eyes the color of a stormy sea, broad shoulders glistening, muscles in his biceps flexing as he thrust. His unspoiled bandage winking in the light. His hand trailed between their bodies, his fingers circling the nub that would provide her boundless gratification.

"If you can, come with me *now*," he urged and lowered to suck her nipple between his teeth.

And she was lost.

Pleasure ripped through her, a sensory explosion. He swallowed her cry, covering her lips with his own as they worked together, clutching and biting and gasping, ringing every drop of gratification from the moment. His breath scorched her skin, the sentiments flowing into her ear both tender and frantic. With a final gasping kiss to her brow, he pulled out and rolled to his side, completing outside her body.

Wave after wave crested as she struggled to catch her breath. Her skin tingled, and she swept her hand over her breasts and down her belly to halt the tremors. Her vision blurred, so she closed her eyes. There was no need trying to gather *anything* beyond air.

When she collected her thoughts, she whispered, "Disengaging was the proper plan." A logical decision, the best decision. Yet, she wished they were still joined. Startled by the thought, she turned her head to find his turning toward her. *My, he was gorgeous*, every disheveled, sweaty inch of him. And he smelled like heaven. *They* smelled like heaven.

He was silent for a pensive moment. Then he

sighed, angled his arm around her and dragged her against him. Into the nook between his shoulder and rib, where she fit quite nicely. Quite perfectly. "A baby would be a muddle, wouldn't it?" he finally asked.

She listened to his heartbeat relax its bounding rhythm, the realization that she'd never felt this connected to another human being crashing down upon her. "Unquestionably."

But she comprehended, and maybe he did, too, that she was lying.

"I think you broke the skin." Caleb peered at the heel of his palm. "Remind me not to get in the way of your pleasure, countess."

Macy took his hand, shifted it into the firelight. There was a faint mark. She didn't know why she'd tried to contain herself by biting him when no one could hear them above the roar of the surf slapping the wharf. "Many apologies for my enthusiasm, sir."

He presented a lopsided grin and handed her an apple slice, his beloved dimple pinging to life. Devilish charm on full display. "I *like* your enthusiasm."

They sat before a stone hearth in a makeshift sitting area outside his bedroom. He'd organized a hasty picnic, producing cheese, apples, crackers. And ale that tasted so good she wanted to guzzle it. A veritable feast when one's strength had been exhausted making love. Three sessions, with brief naps in between. *Three.* Each better than the last, if she could propose such an outlandish thing.

He'd pulled on his breeches, and he sat across from her, knees bent, amber firelight rippling over his face and chest. She wore his shirt. An impulsive decision. And she'd known he liked her wearing it because he'd come in, arms loaded with food, and when he saw her, he halted so suddenly he almost tripped.

Blinked hard while he stared—and she had just *known* he liked it.

He munched on a cracker, tilted his head. Tousled hair, lips swollen from use, cheeks rosy, he presented a handsome portrait. "Can I ask you a question?"

She drew her legs up and rested her chin atop her knees. "Uh-oh. That's always the start of a question I don't want to answer."

He swallowed, took a sip of ale. "This is true. And I'm fishing, prying, which I usually don't. Forget I asked, probably for the best."

"Oh, heavens, ask."

He opened his mouth, hesitated. Silence reigned as he gathered his thoughts. Finally: "Who hurt you?"

Startled, she bumped her head on the wooden crate she rested against. *How did he know?* Her uncle's face flashed before her eyes, and she wrapped her arms around her legs and squeezed. "It was a long time ago. Or so it seems now."

"No denial, then." His fist clenched around the glass. "Your eyes, the way you watched me the first time I touched you. Like you were preparing for battle. Elle had a student a couple of years ago. There was abuse…and something about you, something in the way you reacted, reminded me of her."

She blew out a breath. *Where to start*? "My father was a doctor, too. Did I tell you that?"

He shook his head and took another drink, his gaze focused on her.

"Anyway, his dream was to one day give his practice to his son. My mother tried. Four failed births before I came along." She rubbed her chin on her knee. Wiggled her toes and recorded the dance of firelight over them. "I wanted his love, and when I realized gaining it was unattainable, I worked to gain his respect. I went on house calls with him, and lo and behold, found I had a talent for medicine. I could read a text and close my eyes and still see the words, so studying was effortless. Pictures, diagrams, charts. He was in practice with his brother, and I assumed I would join them. However, my father soundly rejected my proposal, telling me a women's hospital was the place for me." She trailed her foot over a knothole in the floor. The wood was luscious and gleamed in the light thrown from the gas sconce. "So, I turned to my uncle. This when I was around sixteen. I needed training, an internship of sorts, to get accepted into any recognized pre-medical program. He was patient. A middling doctor but a satisfactory teacher. He had no children, no wife. His life revolved around his profession."

Caleb took her hand and pressed a kiss to the inside of her wrist. "And…"

"And then it revolved around me."

His gaze shot to hers. "Your *uncle*?"

She linked their fingers, amazed the simple act could calm her so. "It started with casual touches. Inadvertent. He was apologetic. At first. Then he started making inappropriate comments. Then both. The way he looked at me, ah…it made my stomach turn. But I was young…and foolish. Unaware, to a point. He was my uncle, after all. I found him in my darkened bedchamber on one occasion, which is when I started locking my door and shoving my bureau in front of it."

He squeezed her fingers, encouraging in his tender way. He was right, she needed to finish telling him while she could.

"My father believed me to be melodramatic. An irrational female. My mother was powerless or perhaps uninterested. I found another doctor willing to tutor me. Across town, but no matter. Two weeks before I was set to leave for college, he caught me in their office storeroom." She ran her thumb over a scar on Caleb's knuckle, marveling at the tender way such large hands had touched her. "I'd gone there to get gauze, I think. Or a bottle of rubbing alcohol. A neighbor with a badly infected cut I had promised to treat."

Caleb released an anxious breath. "Macy, he didn't. Because you were…"

"He didn't, Cale." She cupped his cheek, sighed, dropped her hand. Maybe he'd think differently of her after hearing this. "But to stop him…well, I had—I used a scalpel on the table he shoved me into. I caught him beneath his chin. The wound was horrific. He'd roughed me up in the process, torn my clothing, so when I ran into the street, covered in blood, mine and his, looking exactly like what I was, someone who had been assaulted, it was a disaster. A scandal my family never recovered from."

"The police?"

"Oh, yes. It hit the newspapers, too. Such intrigue! My family was prominent in the community, that sort of thing. And, somehow, it was my fault in the eyes of most. I had asked for his mishandling by the way I dressed or my openly affectionate manner. I believe the reporter called it 'behavior indecorous enough to drive a prominent physician to lurid recklessness.' My father moved his practice out of town. He and my uncle died two years later, months apart. I never spoke to either of them again. The worst of it was, he took something from me. Nothing so concrete as my virtue. My innocence, I suppose, which sounds trite. My ability to trust. Except for medicine, he changed my view of my future. Of myself. My mother had a distant cousin who lived here, so after university—" She wiggled her toes, wishing for the heat of his body. "Now there's no one. Just me."

He rounded his arm around her waist and dragged her against him. Smoothed his lips over the crown of her head. A nurturing soul, he'd have made an excellent physician. "Why would you want to talk to them ever again? The bastards."

She laughed and drew back to look at him. There were tiny creases beside his eyes she'd not noticed before. Like lines drawn in the sand. Another item for her treasure chest. How to catalogue everything about this wonderful man in the short time they had? "It's that simple, yes?"

Without comment, he released her and presented his back, squatting before the fire. Grabbed a poker and worked it through the wood and ash in the hearth. To keep from greedily recording the shift of lean muscle and sinew, she looked to the window, surprised to see a purple and crimson wash coloring the horizon. Her heart squeezed. Sunrise was upon them. The end of their magical night. As if he sensed her mournful reflection, his gaze reconnected with hers. "Nothing involving family is simple, even if it looks that way to the ones with their faces pressed to the pane."

"Your family—"

"They're my *world*." He turned on one heel, a violent movement, his hand going to the floor for balance. "But sharing blood means *nothing*, Macy. Or not all, anyway. And I know for a doctor, that's a hard statement to take in. Biology doesn't always win out." He tapped his chest. "Take this advice into your heart, not your head. Some people need to be set adrift, put in a boat that will never again meet yours, and sent out to sea."

"Your father," she whispered. It wasn't a blind guess; she'd heard the rumors.

He blinked, as if deciding whether to admit it. Then he nodded and tossed the poker aside, where it struck the hearth with a clatter. "He ruined things. His marriage, my childhood. With no consequence attached. His actions, how abusive he was and the decisions my mother made to survive, almost tore Noah away from us."

She shook her head. *Why?*

"He wasn't Noah's father. We had no idea until Elle read my mother's diary. She and I were digging through boxes in the attic, not knowing the chaos we were about to unleash." He drew his finger along a gash in the floorboard. "I was so distraught, because even from the grave, he was still upsetting my life. That's what set me off, not the fact Noah and I were half-brothers, which I could have cared less about. Going in like I do, without thinking, I took my anger out on him, the one person I loved most in the world. So, Noah left in the middle of the night, up north to college, although we didn't know where he'd gone. He didn't come home for ten years, until we reckoned we'd lost him."

"But he's back."

He wiped at a streak of ash on his palm. "Yeah, and we're healing."

She kept herself from crossing to him, understanding as a woman, not a doctor, that telling her might help speed the healing process along. And that he needed space to be able to tell her. "There's more?"

"One year, on Christmas Eve, my father

manhandled my mother. Back when Noah was a baby, and Zach was out piloting. I got in the middle of the struggle, even though I was a pretty little fella still, because someone had to. Her lip was bleeding, her cheek bruised. I don't know, maybe it's when I started feeling so comfortable using my fists. Because, honestly, what I did to my father, going at him like that, felt good. Our relationship was over then, even if he stuck around another year or so. We were both broken. And I was left not knowing what to believe in, who to *be*. It would break Zach's heart if he knew, because he wants to protect us so badly, so he doesn't." He looked to her, placing his trust out there like he had apples for their picnic. "And he's not going to. For some reason, I don't want to tell anyone else, I only want to tell *you*."

Her heart expanded, pulsed, a sluggish, hard thump. She wanted to wrap her arms around that boy, whatever had been done to him, and never let go. Perhaps someday, he would share the full story.

She was doomed. Falling in love. Already there, maybe.

"Is Christabel on one of those boats you've sent out to sea?" she found herself asking. *Gracious, what a question, Mouse.*

He rocked back on his heels, the shock streaking his face laughable. "No, *no*." He snagged his hand through his hair, leaving it in adorable twists on his head. "She's always going to be my friend. It wasn't, it *isn't*, like that. It's whispers in the dark,

Doc. The less and the more. We didn't have them, not at all."

"Care to explain what that means?"

He moved in, the penetrating way he looked at her bringing that frenetic, now-familiar throb between her thighs. *Oh*, what he did to her. "Your hair is wild, sweetheart." She went to tuck, tame, but he captured her hand, lacing their fingers before she could. "I like it crazy. No need to fix it on my account. Not when I'm going to mess it up again before I walk you home."

"I'm confused." She palmed the nape of his neck, slid her fingers into his hair. One hard tug to the strands, which she'd noticed during their adventures he liked. *A lot.* "I thought our night was ending."

He dropped his head back with a moan that sounded like surrender. In the distance, the ferry bell clanged, a reminder of the clock counting off the time they had left. "For a healer, you sure fight dirty. Using what I like against me."

"As if you wouldn't use what I like against me."

With a growl, he yanked her to him. Beneath the thin cotton of his breeches and her shirt, their heated skin merged. Unbelievably, he was hard. Ready for her. And she was ready for him. "Is that a dare?"

She sent him a look she hoped conveyed every erotic impulse directing her mind and body. "If it was, would you take it?"

He laughed and laid her back, his body claiming hers before she took her next breath. "You're damn right I would."

Chapter Six

CALEB DIDN'T HAVE THE LANGUAGE to describe what was happening to him.

How possessed, how *consumed*, he was with someone he'd known mere weeks. How her name circled his mind like a chant. *Macy, Doc, Mouse.* How she made him feel alive and sheltered and confident. How she'd made winter warmer, the sun brighter. Even Christmas was growing on him. He'd found himself humming one of those godawful carols the other day.

Maybe the words wouldn't come—but the feelings *had*.

The quiet collapse of his heart.

So many things had mastered any objection he might have about letting himself fall. When he caught her chewing on her bottom lip as she reviewed medical texts. Pausing at his front door to shake out her crumpled skirt before he walked her home in the dewy darkness. Holding back her laughter, which she did more times than not and for what reason he had no clue. The way she smelled like roses one day and lilacs the next. Her incredible mind, which spun as quickly as the guts of a timepiece. Her slightly crooked smile, one of the few imperfections he had found.

And he'd looked. When one was fascinated, one looked.

Closely.

One night had bled into sixteen, when he wanted his time with her to bleed into the days. So he could come to know her mind as well as he was her body. In the past two weeks, they'd made love all over his house and hers. But mostly in the warehouse, which suited them both the best. Up till dawn, talking and tangling the sheets. Those picnics he was coming to cherish before the fire or sprawled out on his bed.

Besides his heart, really, all he was losing was rest.

He'd fallen asleep in Zach's office yesterday and received a blistering brotherly lecture about burning the candle at both ends. Then Noah had to jump in and tell them where the term came from, which was so dull he'd gone right back to sleep.

Only more frightening than the incredible sex was the fact he was telling Macy things he'd never told another soul. Things that made him feel like a lost little boy while he was doing the telling. The kid who'd been so terrified, so sad.

He crossed his arms and blew out a breath that frosted when it hit air. He was falling in love as surely as Christmas wreaths adorned every door in town. Heck, maybe he'd been there since she kissed him in that cloakroom and turned his world upside down. Love sneaking up out of nowhere and biting him in the ass would be a kick, now, wouldn't it?

What to do about *that*? What to do about *her*?

God sure did have fun with all the situations he put people in.

A resolute gust whipped down the street, nearly taking his hat with it. He caught it before it hit the boardwalk and bumped his way through the door of the mercantile. He was waiting on a final item for Macy's present, and with Christmas only four days away, time was sneaking past. A quick telegram to Raleigh to check on the delivery, then he could get to the warehouse, where his girl had promised to go after she gave medicine to Lilian Quinn's seventeen-year-old, should-already-be-dead cat. Macy had said, while wrapped snugly around his body the night before, that although she was not a veterinarian, animal patients were better than no patients, though he wasn't sure he agreed. Damn fool town. He must have shown twenty people his scar and bragged on how straight and fine it was, *much* better than anything Magnus Leland had ever done. Someone better visit her broken-down office soon and ask for medical attention, or he was going to get irritated. And no one wanted an annoyed Caleb Garrett running around town.

Mr. Scoggins nodded to him from behind the counter but didn't pause sorting ribbons, which were selling by the wagonload with all the gifts to wrap. The scent of peppermint sticks and chocolate stormed him as he made his way to the back of the shop and the combined post and telegraph office. A gaggle of women were there, arranging cards and licking stamps, the feathers on their hats twitching like birds in the throes of death. He rolled his eyes and rocked back on his heels. *Great.*

He wished he'd brought his sketchpad. An idea for a rudder design had come to him on the walk, while he'd been daydreaming about the dainty satin ribbon on Macy's drawers, and he'd like to capture it before it slipped away. The design, that is.

He'd get home soon enough and work on those drawer ribbons.

As the ladies prattled, he ran calculations in his head, practically an expert on ignoring idle chatter. Noah talked more than a girl, always had, and Caleb had long ago gotten used to letting it flitter in one ear and zip out the other. But then they mentioned Macy, and he straightened like someone had lifted him to the balls of his feet by his collar.

"Where did you say the telegram came from?" This from Mrs. Petersen, whose husband owned a whaling boat and was one of Caleb's best customers.

"Philadelphia. A woman's hospital. For women *only.*" Bet Tuppert, who'd put two husbands in the ground and was working on killing number three. "Can you imagine?"

Yes, he could. Macy had mentioned a training program for new doctors. One of the best in the country. *Most competitive*, was exactly how she'd phrased it. His heart stuttered and sank to what felt like his feet. She had gotten accepted.

Considering the expense, no one sent a telegram unless the news was good.

Quitting the mercantile, he stumbled home without feeling the chill ripping through his open coat. He patted his bare head. Left his hat on the telegraph counter. Or maybe he'd dropped it along the way.

It didn't matter. What he'd known was going to happen *was*. Macy was going to leave Pilot Isle and become who she should be. Which was not a brilliant doctor who practiced on half-dead cats. Married to a boatbuilder and living in a rambling house overlooking the sea.

Not her future.

And she, not his.

She was going to leave. And, by God, he was going to let her.

Pack his heart back in his chest for the *last* time and let her.

Macy paced the length of Caleb's workroom, flipping the telegram from one hand to the other like it would singe her skin if she held it for more than a second.

She licked her lips and halted in the center of the room. Unfolded the sheet, bent back the corner over the word *accepted*. Took a deep breath that delivered his intoxicating scent and a dozen sensual recollections. *Practice, Mouse. Don't think about his wondrous hands. His talented lips. How thoughtful he is. How generous. How the ground drops away the moment you see him. Not right now.* "Caleb. Cale. I received a...I mean to say, with regard to the residency program, I would like to propose—" She swore beneath her breath and continued her march to the wall and back. Not *propose.* Men got nervous when a woman used that word. And she wasn't expecting marriage, although most women would at this point.

The details were immaterial. Love wasn't.

I don't want the position in Philadelphia.

I want more. Longer. Forever.

Here. With you.

"I will even help decorate your house, which currently looks like your eight-year-old nephew did the job." *Because I, Elinor Macy Dallas, love you, Caleb Eli Garrett.* Laughing, she spun in a wild circle until she got so dizzy, she had to catch her balance on the hull of his unfinished skiff. The wood was smooth beneath her fingers. Slick, cool. Molten brown in the muted light thrown from the sconce.

Oh, how she appreciated his talent.

It wasn't only boats he was good with, she thought with a wicked smile. If he touched her with so much as his pinky, ownership of her body shifted like a draft deposited in his bank, no longer hers in any way.

Now, it was time to shift ownership of her heart.

She sighed and thrust the telegram in her pocket. *How to tell him?*

But when he arrived, bringing a wintry chill with him, it was obvious someone already had.

She smoothed her hand over wood still serrated in places and tried to suppress a memory that would only complicate the discussion. Two nights ago, holding on to this very section of the boat with Caleb standing behind her, thrusting in the most leisurely motion he was able to maintain, or so he'd whispered against her shoulder, deliberateness she'd begged for release from. It had been the most erotic night of her life. Beyond anything she'd ever dreamed she would share with a man. Beyond who she thought she could be. "Let me guess. Someone read my telegram." She gave the hull a soft tap when she felt like racing to him. Unexpectedly, and for one of the first times, he looked unapproachable. "Small town charms."

He closed the door and leaned against it. Crossed his ankles and his arms, closing himself off. Slipping away like fog over the inlet. "You want to hear something I now find pretty damn amusing?" He ran his hand over the stubble dotting his jaw. The man shaved in the morning and by noon, needed to shave again. She particularly loved the feel of his whiskers abrading her thighs.

"What?" she asked, though she was relatively sure she didn't want to know.

"When we started this, I figured if I touched you, it'd release the pressure building since you kissed me in that cloakroom. Erase the need like words from one of Elle's blackboards. One swipe and poof"—he snapped his fingers—"gone."

She thrust her hand in her pocket and crushed the telegram. "The residency. I'm not taking it."

He shoved off the door and crossed the room until the boat was all that was standing between them. "Oh, yes, you are," he growled and slapped his hand atop it.

Her heart shattered as she gazed in his eyes. They'd gone the color of smoke, which meant thoughts, and stubbornness, were running deep. "You'd deny what you feel? You'd send me away like this?"

"I'm not denying anything. That's why you're going to accept."

"I don't *want* the position, Cale. *I want you.*"

A muscle in his jaw flexed. He closed his eyes and drew the hand lying atop the boat into a fist. "I'm all wrong for you. And I hate to tell you, but you're all wrong for *me*. I'm a simple boatbuilder. I get irritated easily. I'm not tolerant. I'm not anything you need. I won't be good for you. Smart enough for you." He banged his hand on the hull. "And I don't know how to be."

"You're everything—"

He snarled and stepped in, rocking the skiff into her. "My mother believed my father was everything, Doc. And it was *never* true. I'm not repeating the past. Not when I've worked my whole life to avoid it. And I'm not holding you back from a future you're supposed to have. One *you've* worked for. Or have you forgotten?"

"All I remember is being utterly alone in the world before you. Alone, Cale, *no one.* You have family, so you can't begin to understand." She tried to snag his sleeve as he brushed past her. "You'll not only allow your father to ruin your childhood but this…" Her words slipped away as she gestured wildly to the two of them.

He paused by a stack of shipping crates serving as an informal sideboard, grabbed a bottle of whiskey and a chipped glass. "I choose to think of it as taking the only education the bastard gave me and putting it to good use." He poured generously. "Why the anger? We agreed, this was temporary. It had to end sometime. You don't belong here. Your future is bigger than Pilot Isle."

"Those were *your* rules. My agreement was misinterpreted."

He downed a swallow of whiskey, glanced at her over his shoulder. The iciness of his gaze leached into her bones. Steadfast, a slight tremor in his hand was his only tell. "Fine, they're my rules."

She walked forward, tobacco and the spicy tang that was Caleb's alone soaking her senses as blood would gauze. She caught her breath as awareness wrapped them like a gift. As she flushed, head to toe, perspiration dewing her skin. She wasn't going to let him do this. He was kind, complicated, loyal. A gifted artist. A man who loved with great intensity but was unable to accept love in return. She wanted him for all those things.

Loved him for all of them.

She guessed sending her to Philadelphia was *his* way of loving.

He drained the last of the whiskey. "Don't do

this," he warned.

She pushed her coat off her shoulders, her gaze locked to his as it dropped to the floor. Yanked her shirtwaist from her skirt. Was manipulating the bone buttons down the front when she heard his glass hit the floor. With a muttered oath, he lifted her off her feet, leaving her slippers behind. Five paces until they met the wall, which he crowded her into without finesse, his body a hard, heated press.

Then he ravaged.

Within moments, their clothing littered the heart pine planks. He brought her down atop the heap, tangling his hand in her hair and tilting her head to bring the kiss to a cavernous level. His hands roamed her body, doing everything she loved. Teeth on her nipple, fingers delving inside her. Mere seconds, and she was aflame. Writhing, panting, moaning. Intertwined, she wasn't sure where she left and he started, so when he lifted her hips and surged inside, she experienced nothing but joy. Unadulterated, mindless joy.

Pleasure.

Waves and waves gushing through her as she screamed, sank her nails in his back and held him as she rode it out. Desire was blinding, wondrous, incalculable. However, when he paused mid-stroke and looked deeply into her eyes, cradled her face and whispered *I love you*, she should have recognized he was saying goodbye.

Two agonizing days later, Caleb gripped the ferry railing as the vessel made a gentle turn toward Pilot Isle's dockside and the roofline of his warehouse popped into view. Settled against a glorious backdrop of azure sky and foam-capped surf, the sight of the treasured structure he'd built with his own hands brought no pleasure. A moist gust stung his cheeks and slipped inside his coat, chilling a body already frozen from the inside out.

A heart frozen from the inside out.

He tugged his hat low and gazed into the churning gray froth, drew a breath tasting of woodsmoke and the sea. He needed a drink, or five. Leaving Macy in his bed and sneaking out at dawn had been cowardly—and probably the biggest mistake of his life.

Refusing that residency would be the biggest mistake of hers.

At least he'd left a *note*. One he'd carefully composed while watching her sleep, about the most painful goddamn sentiment he'd ever put to paper. Although he had a gut feeling his hastily written missive might have made her angry when he'd only been trying to explain. Balance out telling her he loved her and why he thought she should leave him in the same breath.

The bell clanged to announce the ferry's arrival, and Caleb lifted his head, scanning the wharf with his heart in his throat. Maybe…just maybe…

Nope, she wasn't there. Only people waiting were a crowd of fishermen with their gear thrown over their shoulders, looking to hitch the next crossing back to the mainland. After what he'd said to her, Macy wasn't likely to be waiting on him ever again.

Being away from her for fifty-five hours had proven one thing, he didn't want to be alone anymore.

But he'd gone and messed up the perfect relationship with the perfect woman, so he was sure as hell going to be. Because Macy was *it* for him. He didn't want anyone else, would never want anyone else. She made him feel like the luckiest man in the world. However, he couldn't live with her remorse, if she had any about choosing him. So he'd given her up. If he'd had the courage to fight for her, she might well be standing on that warped dock right now, her hair glistening in the sun, that keen gaze trained on him in a way that made him feel like the only person in her universe.

He could hold her hand as they walked home, as he told her about his trip, and his agreement to build five new boats for a dealer in Raleigh who was selling them quicker than Caleb could roll them out. He needed to hire two more builders to complete the order—and this should have made him very happy.

Instead, he felt like he'd never be happy again.

CHAPTER SEVEN

MACY REALIZED THE PEOPLE SUR-
ROUNDING her as she sobbed on their
upholstered settee were part of the Garrett package. If she forced the stubborn ass she was in love
with to realize he was not only good enough for
her but *exactly* what she wanted, what she *needed*,
she also got his family.

His adorable, argumentative, tenacious, devoted
family.

Family. The word, so long denied, made her
heart clutch. Made a fresh wave of tears streak
her cheeks. When she wasn't a crier, had never
been a crier. *Oh, how she hated Caleb Garrett!* She'd
sniffled all the way down Main Street, garnering
more than her fair share of looks. Well, she'd tell
those old biddies that waking up alone after being
told you were loved for the first time was *very bad
indeed.* For two days, she'd tried to process the
situation and find a sensible solution.

Find a way to claim her man.

In an overbearing show of masculine high-
handedness, which was horribly unlike Caleb, he'd
left a note listing all the reasons she was going to
take the residency, then snuck out before sunrise
like a rat. Blind rage had lasted about five minutes

as she stomped about the warehouse looking for objects to break, then abject wretchedness kicked in when she found a sketch of her slipped in a hidden nook of his desk.

Still a weeping, pathetic mess two days later, she'd sought out her only friends. Who unfortunately happened to be the coward's sisters. In-law. *Damn small towns*, she seethed. *Damn you, Caleb Garrett.* When she got her hands on—

"Let's start at the beginning." Elle uncurled Macy's clenched fist. "I'm sorry to say, as a preface to anything you tell us: the Garrett men are known for mucking things up, however brilliant and handsome they may be."

"He left...a note. A *note!*" Macy ripped the waded sheet from her pocket and threw it to the floor. The vellum was moist from her tears, which brought a renewed flood of fury. If she ever saw the man again, she was either going to kiss him or kill him. Maybe both. She certainly couldn't murder him *here*, in a house resembling a Sears, Roebuck & Co. Christmas advertisement. Gorgeous tree. Garland looped around every post. The scent of cinnamon and nutmeg riding the air. At any moment, someone was going to press a warm cookie into her hand, she just knew it.

Savannah went to one knee and smoothed the note on the settee. She raised a brow as she mouthed the words while she read. "He bought you a train ticket to Philadelphia?"

"Ah..." Elle pressed a handkerchief into Macy's hand. "You got the residency."

"I'm not taking it!" She waved the slip of embroidered linen like a flag. "Even if I never talk to him again, and I have to give enemas to Lilian Quinn's cats for the rest of my life, I'm not leaving. The train departed this morning, with me not on it! I'll haunt him, that's what. Or put spiders in his bed. Spiders will show him!"

Savannah contained her smile, but just. "What is this about Lilian's cats and *enemas?*"

"He told you about the spiders?" Elle questioned, her brows split by a neat fold of bewilderment. As if the conversation was taking a turn she had not expected.

"He told me a lot of things," she said and dropped her head to her hands. In the distance, the ferry bell clanged. Maybe Caleb was on that boat, but he wasn't sailing back to face her. *I'm staying in Raleigh until after your train departs*, the note had clarified, should she think the coming nights were theirs. As the sixteen before had been. *Don't make this harder, please.* He hadn't written the plea but had whispered it as she fell asleep in his arms.

Truthfully, waking alone had not been that immense a surprise.

The door to the parlor opened, and the stomp of boots sounded. Macy lifted her head to see Noah enter the room with Zach behind him.

"Where's the fire?" Zach asked and wedged his shoulder against the doorframe. "Oh, crazy me. That'd be the one Rory lit in the backyard. The one I had a devil of a time putting out." He dragged his arm across his brow, sending a streak of ash across his skin. "That boy is going to be the death of me. This better be important, my lovelies. God knows what he's gotten into in the last five minutes."

Savannah brought Caleb's awful, tear-stained note to her lips and smiled behind it. "All boys start fires from time to time, of some sort or another. We should encourage his inquisitive nature, not try so decidedly to contain it."

"Yeah, yeah." Zach frowned, but the look he sent his wife singed the air. "You and your affectionate discipline are turning him into a hellion. Just like his mother. Damn, I hope Regina takes after me, or I may not live to meet my grandbabies."

Noah fit his long body in the armchair opposite Macy and gave his spectacles a nudge. "Let me guess. You have a confounding case on which you'd like to collaborate, although I don't know why a medical mystery would bring you to tears. In any case, one scientist to another, we shall collaborate. Because, sadly, we're the only two in town. Except that ass, Leland. I'm not a doctor of medicine, true, but I love research almost as much as I love"—he jacked his thumb Elle's way—"her."

Oh, had Caleb been correct about his adorably intellectual younger brother. "I'm sorry, Dr. Garrett, I need a scientist who understands love, not fish."

Noah slumped back in the chair. "I'm entirely confused."

"Nothing new there, darling," Elle said and

slid into his lap like she'd done it a hundred times before. Savannah had moved beside Zach, and they'd laced fingers. Macy observed them, envious. A voyeur to a life she wanted but might never have. The Garretts were pieces of each other's puzzles.

And it took each locked in place to make a family.

Savannah held the note before Zach's face. He wrinkled his nose, squinted. Held out his hand to Noah, who sighed as he surrendered his spectacles. "You really need to keep yours in your pocket, Constable," Noah muttered.

Zach fit a metal arm over each ear, then took the missive. Caleb was right about him, too, Macy concluded. The patriarch. The problem-solver. *Even if he doesn't want to solve them*, Caleb had acknowledged during one of their impromptu picnics.

"He told her about the spiders," Elle said as if *that* bit of silliness was significant.

Zach pressed his lips together to hold back a smile. Folded the note with neat tucks and handed it to Savannah. "Color me shocked."

A blaze fueled behind Macy's breastbone. Ire directed at a Garrett, but not the foolhardy one she loved to the depths of her soul. "Shocked. Of course." She tossed the handkerchief to the settee and leapt to her feet. "*This* is the problem. He doesn't believe he's good enough. For anyone in this room. He thinks you're"—she pointed at Noah—"the intellectual. And you're"—Zach—

"the saint. And his father the monster *he* resembles. Heavens! Has anyone ever taken the time to tell him he's wrong?"

Noah choked like he'd taken a blow to his solar plexus. "He told you about his father?"

Zach lifted from the doorframe. "Well, this answers the question of who my cantankerous baby brother is going to end up with."

"Don't count on it," Macy whispered, "because he doesn't understand."

Elle tilted her head. "Understand what?"

"He's an *artist*. Gifted beyond measure. Caring and dependable and considerate. And, yes, somewhat belligerent. Dreadfully stubborn. Setting broken bones is more fun than arguing with the man." She gained steam as his family stared, blinding smiles lighting their faces. "This entire town has left him feeling like he's inferior. When he's *not*. He's perfect. For me, anyway. And I *want* him." She exhaled and collapsed to the settee. "Also, lest you think he started this, *I* did."

Noah released a muted gust of laughter, then tried to wipe his face clean when he realized she'd heard it.

"Someone needs to make him understand." Macy scooted to the edge of the cushion and sent Noah the somber look she employed before cutting someone open. "And you're just the Garrett to do it."

Caleb removed the sail from the halyard and ran

his finger over the shackle. They were new ones he'd ordered from a supplier in Maine, and he wasn't sure he liked them. The bolts were a little wide, maybe not the best fit with the grommets his sailmaker preferred. He groaned and stretched, looked at the material puddled like spilled milk around his feet. It reminded him of making love to Macy atop their twisted pile of clothing. Right on this spot, three horrendously forlorn days ago.

Goddammit. He crossed the room, heading for a whiskey bottle he knew wouldn't solve his problems. With his luck, he'd drink too much, slice his finger open angling that hull and have to beg, *beg*, Magnus Leland to attend to him.

Glass in hand, he tossed back a shot, the liquid stinging his throat but providing some measure of comfort.

It wouldn't last.

Not when Macy occupied every nook and crevice of his mind, his heart. His home. His warehouse. The scent of lilacs and memories crowded each corner. Of her eyes flooding sapphire when pleasure took her. Of her running her thumb across his wrist as he told her all the stories he'd bottled up for so long. He'd never had a real friend outside his brothers. A person he wanted to tell, well, *everything.* Not even Christabel. Loneliness was tearing at him until he wondered if he'd ever crawl away from it. Why, this morning he'd found Macy's hairclip tucked beneath his counterpane, and for a long moment, he'd wondered if he was going to cry.

The jolt of anguish had nearly knocked him from his feet.

Only so much pressure you could put on even the finest quality sail. Folds and creases stressed the fibers until they broke, and he was beginning to feel stressed to the limit. Close to breaking.

She hadn't used the train ticket. This he knew. His lady doctor was still here, maybe missing him as much as he was missing her. Probably mad as a hornet, too.

Which he guessed meant he needed to make it up to her.

Tell her he didn't want her to go to Philadelphia, even if it *was* the adventure of a lifetime. The start of an amazing career. His fear of her regretting it one day, being *sorry* she chose him—and a modest medical practice in a town it was going to take time to win over—was the lone thing keeping him from breaking down her door. That, and the thought of her having to practice on those cats.

Going home to his achingly solitary house was breaking his heart in two. Macy was the one for him. It was no longer a question, if it ever had been. If he could only find the courage to claim her. To *tell* her. "Coward," he whispered and whipped his glass at the wall, droplets of whiskey staining his sketches and trailing to the floor in rivulets. Like he'd told her, he ruined things. It was a family tradition.

"Whoa!" Noah danced aside to avoid the spray of glass as he shot through the doorway. Frowning, he stepped over the carnage. "Your temper is a sight to behold, Cale, it truly is."

Caleb yanked his hand through his hair. *Great.* "You lose the bet? Or Zach chicken out? Giving advice is usually his job."

"Boy, do you have it wrong. I'm here under doctor's orders." Noah held his hand chest high. "Yea tall. Blonde. Dictatorial. Good with a needle, thread, and torn skin. Remember her?"

Caleb knelt next to the sail and began a haphazard job of folding it. Kept his hands busy, maybe, but it was frankly a two-person job. More if you were trying to complete the task on a deck or over the lifelines onto the dock. Noah went to the other end and stretched the material taut.

"Stack the luff on top of the tack, Professor, or it'll stretch down the length of the bag."

Noah snapped the cloth. "How many times do you think I've done this? Larger folds on the tack end and smaller folds at the clew. Pretty simple geometric principles in play. Angles and diameter. I think I have it."

"Amazing. You can even make folding a sail sound boring."

Noah paused, tilted his head in thought. "This is actually an advantageous ingress into the conversation. I *am* boring. But Elle doesn't see me that way. She sees me in a way I don't see myself, Cale. And didn't for a long time. Sometimes still don't when I look in the mirror, truth be told."

Caleb did a quick pleat. Too quick. He sighed and adjusted it. "Everyone knows about your fascinating love story. Attached since you were children, made for each other. And if they didn't, her carving *Elle loves Noah* into all those oaks kept it for, what would you call it, posterity?"

"As usual, you're missing the point. I left Pilot Isle because finding out my father wasn't the same one you and Zach shared changed the way I thought about myself. And there was Elle with her starry eyes and, yes, her decimated tree trunks, expecting me to be her champion when I'd lost my way. Completely. I couldn't save her when I had mislaid myself. But I could have stayed— and I think she would have helped me find the answers long before I did. Painfully, and on my own. Apart from everyone I loved."

Caleb lined up the edge of the sail, shadowing Noah's movement. "You ran away, you mean," he whispered, still irritated over an issue they had mostly settled when Noah returned last year.

"Thought we worked through my leaving, Cale."

Caleb shot a glance at his brother, took in the light winking off his spectacles, the solemn gray eyes so like his own. The tug to his heartstrings was expected. He and Zach were as close as brothers could be, but somehow, it was Noah who got to him. Always had. Like Macy did, in a way. The pleasure and pain of insurmountable love. "We did," he muttered and threw his concentration back to the sail, "you know that."

Noah worked to contain the middle folds as they closed in on completing the job. "Start a war with yourself over this, if you must, but you won't win. I tried, believe me. Wasted ten years. Without Elle, without you. Zach, Rory."

Caleb took the sail from Noah and shoved it in the bag, destroying half of what they'd accomplished. "Doctor's orders, huh?" he asked, keeping his gaze nailed to the floor. The flush sweeping his face was not one he was disclosing to his baby brother.

Noah walked to the wall of sketches, trailed his finger over a roughly drawn cutter. "Why not accept the way she sees you? Maybe she's right." He traced the lines, bow to stern. "Very determined. Reminds me of Elle when she has the bit between her teeth. Downright fearsome, the intensity. Love provides a microscopic view, a viewpoint Macy is quite experienced with, I should add. Science requires one who is comfortable examining the details."

Caleb's heart gave three hard knocks. She loved him, and she'd admitted it. *To his family.* "I told her I loved her, if you think that's the problem. You and Zach misplaced the most critical information, and I remembered the confusion. Getting a woman to listen when it's basically too late has got to be the hardest ask on the planet. So, I admitted it, flat-out. And she…" The glimmer in her eyes when he'd whispered those words would *never* leave his mind. "She heard me."

Noah settled his long body against the wall. "Hooray. You're more than halfway there," he said and gave a slow clap. "With all the packages arriving from Raleigh, Atlanta, New

York, I suspect there's an incredible gift in there somewhere. The foundation, not the whole, mind you, of an amazingly humble apology. Tomorrow's Christmas, if you haven't checked the calendar of late. You're right on time, if a gross display of supplication is on the docket."

Caleb gave the sail bag a shove with his boot. "Supplication your fancy word for begging?"

"Absolutely."

Caleb looked to the window. Periwinkle and a buttery gold were painting a dimming sky. If he closed his eyes, he could hear the sea rolling into shore. The squawk of a seagull as it searched the wharf for scraps of food. A sail snapping in the wind. The sounds he'd heard every day of his life. *She* was the change in how he was starting to feel about himself. She was the difference. "I'm just learning to like myself, and she thinks I'm perfect already."

"Perfect for *her*, Cale. That's the magic. I'm a scientist, but in this case, I'll tell you, don't deconstruct. Accept it. Trust her. Trust *yourself*."

"Faith," Caleb whispered when he was mostly a faithless man. Sliding his hand in his pocket, he brushed his fingers over her hairclip. Experienced the same ache he did when he watched Rory cross a crowded street; watched Zach head out on patrol with those goddamned shipwrecks. The same ache he'd felt after seeing Noah for the first time in ten years.

Like a sucker punch, love had the power to bring you to your knees when you weren't looking.

"Get Macy to your house tomorrow. Tell her Rory cut his foot, and he's bleeding like a stuck pig. That will work." Caleb rocked back on his heels, making a mental list of what needed to be done. It was, maybe, a decent start to his pleading for her forgiveness. For her *future*. "I need tonight, maybe all night. Don't bungle this, Professor."

Noah tipped his head to the ceiling, trying to hide the curve of his lips. *The bastard.* "The gift, I'm guessing."

Caleb was halfway out the door when he remembered to look back. "And...thanks. You know—"

Noah waved away the words. "I know, Cale. I've always known."

Love, Caleb decided as he stalked down the boardwalk, was the best and the hardest of things.

CHAPTER EIGHT

" ARE YOU MAD? THAT I don't need no doctor?" Rory perched his skinny bottom next to hers on the top porch stair. He'd brought the aroma of the holidays with him. Cinnamon and nutmeg. Peppermint, from the sugar stick in his hand. In the other, he held a wooden caboose. He looked like his father, Zach. A spitting image. "It's one of those lies that don't hurt anyone. What Elle told me. A yellow lie. But it wasn't funny, if you ask me. Like a good joke or something."

"White lie. And, no, I'm surprised. A tad nervous." She drew her shawl around her shoulders to fend off the gust whipping past them. The air tasted of salt and rain and Christmas, which she supposed was Pilot Isle's own unique mix. "But not mad."

"Uncle Cale loves you. So, you gotta stay 'til he gets here."

She smiled, casting her gaze to the sky. Brilliant blue. Full of possibilities, a sky this wide open. "Is that so?"

"The out-and-out plan, my pa said."

"Your family is quite the plotting bunch."

Rory shoved the peppermint stick in his mouth. Moved it from one side to the other. "Plotting mean crazy?" he asked around the red and white swirls.

She laughed, flooded with hope, wonder, love. Brushing Rory's hair from his brow, she allowed her hand to linger as the softness of his skin blended with her own. The little boy scent of him aimed an arrow straight at her heart. "Yes, maybe."

Then Caleb was there. Windblown and rosy-cheeked, broad and tall and wonderful. Striding down the sidewalk and through the gate. Taking her hand and pulling her into his arms. The kiss was swift, child-friendly, but generated enough heat to make her lose all coherent thought.

"She's not mad, Uncle Cale," Rory mumbled around the candy, his lips turning a charming pink. "But she thinks we're crazy."

Caleb's brow rose. Just the one, which she found incredibly endearing. And he knew it. "Not angry? Then maybe you don't want the gift I've been busting my—"

"Oh, no. Don't even! You have so much groveling to do, I can't begin to tell you. After you made me wait four day in misery, Caleb Garrett, I should never speak to you again."

"But you will." He pulled her down the sidewalk with a wave over his shoulder. "Too cold out here for visiting, boy. Get inside. We'll be back by supper."

"Thanks for the train, Uncle Cale. Merry Christmas, Doc Dallas!" Rory shouted as the screen door slapped behind him.

She didn't speak on the hasty walk through

town. Christmas morning, so the streets were deserted. Caleb's fingers were laced tightly with hers when a strong hold wasn't necessary. She wasn't going *anywhere*. "I sent a telegram. I declined the residency. No matter what—"

"God, I missed you," he whispered and captured her in his hold, right there in the street. This kiss was unlike the earlier one regulated for Rory's viewing. This was carnal—and warmed her to her toes. When he raised his head, he was breathing as if he'd run a race. "Your Christmas gift or more of this at the warehouse? We're gonna do both, but your choice which we do first." He trailed his knuckle across her cheek. "You know what I'll say."

She tapped her finger over her scorched lips, her body vibrating with need so compellingly she truly questioned the decision. While she wanted the warehouse *more*, she also wanted to make him suffer. "Gift, first. Ripping each other's clothes off, second. Maybe."

He pressed his lips to her brow and groaned. "Women." But he was smiling, his dimple denting his cheek, the wicked look in his eyes making her knees weak.

When they arrived at his warehouse—which she thought meant he'd reneged and was opting for lovemaking first—he circled behind it. To a modest structure she'd assumed was used for storage as she'd not been invited inside. It was newly painted. White clapboard. Bright blue shingles. Cedar roof. Pristine, solid, and quite appealing standing there in a ripping wind flowing off the sea. The sign, *her* sign—Elinor Macy Dallas, Medical Doctor—was hanging on a new hook, not yet rusted, the first hint to what she'd find inside.

At the entrance, he halted, blew in his hands, danced from one foot to the other. Struggling, she plainly noted. She laughed and elbowed him aside, opened the door and stepped right back into him as he came through it. "Caleb," she breathed. *Oh, my.*

"Merry Christmas," he said and gave her backside a shove. "Go on, explore. Before you decide about me, about us, I want to sweeten the deal. I'm not fighting fair, I guess. But if you're not going to have that residency, you're going to have everything else."

She orbited the room like a star circling a planet, staying close to her center. *Him.* Medical cabinets spanned the entire length of one wall, the glass shelves filled with all manner of instrument. Stethoscope, anesthesia inhaler, irrigating syringes, lancets, scalpels. Bottles of antiseptic. Ointment. Jars of cotton balls, pads, gauze. It was as well stocked as any physician's office she had ever seen.

"Where did you…" Iron cylinder, glass bulbs, metal electrodes. She touched the x-ray machine in wonder while envisioning what she could do with it. Setting broken bones without guessing where the break was and having additional knowledge for surgeries would be the most remarkable advance of her medical career.

Caleb left his post by the door. "Only one for a hundred miles. Exposure in ninety minutes, which I think means it's good. Let Magnus Leland try to get one, the rat bastard. I had to promise to design a skiff for the hospital chief to even be able to place the order."

She ran her finger over the oblong cylinder. "Crookes tube. A recent discovery. 1895. First used to locate bullets embedded in the body. My father didn't have an x-ray machine, never dreamed of having one, I imagine."

"You and Noah can have long discussions about tubes and scientific discoveries. Bore yourself to tears. Once he knows you have this thing, he'll make your life a living hell. He'll start operating on people if you let him."

"Caleb…" She turned and pinned him with what she hoped was a penetrating gaze and not a lovesick one. "You have the money for this?"

He chewed on the inside of his cheek. "The boat business is going really well."

"Should I be afraid of what you've put in the other room?"

"Surgical chair. Converts to a table for the exceedingly ghastly things you do to a body. Got it in Indiana. Best on the market." At her questioning look, he continued, "I have a client in Morehead City. A doctor who loves spending money on sailboats. He helped me outfit this place, most I have no idea what it's even used for. And I honestly don't want to from the hideous names alone."

"Caleb—"

"I know you'd have a whole hospital full of equipment in Philadelphia. If you're determined to stay in Pilot Isle, even if you don't marry me"—his eyes changed color, a flood of ashen gray—"I want you to have this office. Be the doctor you were meant to be. That you've *trained* to be."

She stepped in, bounced up on her toes, and threw her arms around him—just like that time in the cloakroom. Pressed her cheek to his chest as his wild heartbeat stampeded through her, no stethoscope required. "Why would I stay, working right behind your warehouse, if I *didn't* marry you?"

"Because you're too good for me." He kissed the top of her head and drew her close. "But I make a mean cup of coffee and pretty good biscuits, which you should recall from our midnight picnics. You'd be over here all the time anyway. And I have no doctor except you to treat my numerous injuries. Boatbuilding is hazardous at times. Or I'm clumsy, take your pick. I hope I'm gradually working my way up to a family discount."

"I love you, Caleb Garrett," she said, the words muffled in the folds of his shirt. He and his family were, quite simply, the answer to her prayers. "So much that I'm having trouble believing I found you."

"Say it again," he whispered. "I don't think I'll ever tire of hearing it."

She did, once, twice, until he stopped her when

his lips captured hers. A kiss to stop clocks, she would tell her grandchildren one day.

He tipped her gaze to his. "You're sure? As in, Dr. Elinor Macy *Garrett* sure. The answer better be yes, or I'm out a new sign." He flushed, and her heart stuttered. "Top drawer, by the x-ray."

She retreated from his hold and opened the drawer. Inside lay the new sign. And shoved in a back corner, sat a crimson velvet box. With trembling hands, she picked it up.

"The town jeweler's been pestering me about a new boat, so we negotiated an earlier delivery date if he opened up on Christmas Eve, special circumstances and all that. Elle helped me pick it out. She said it was the most fun she's had all year." Caleb yanked a glove off and slapped it against his thigh. His voice shook, just a little, but she heard it. "Which says a lot about Noah, and not much of it good."

She held her arm out, the box perfectly centered on her open palm. She chased his gaze around the room, delighted by his bashfulness. "Time to finish the job. I don't believe I heard a question."

Tucking his glove in his armpit, he took the box from her. It looked tiny in his hand, but he popped the top back with nary a stumble, like he'd practiced. He smiled shyly, his gaze finally meeting hers when she let out a breathless sigh. "It's not a question, but marry me, and I'll spend my life making sure you know how much I love you. Making sure you don't regret it."

She reached, then drew her hands back and

twisted them together. Her heartbeat was drumming in her chest loud enough for him to hear. It would not be helpful if she fainted during the proposal. "Oh, Cale. It's beautiful." Simple. Elegant. Stunning. A round sapphire surrounded by a circle of diamonds, the most beautiful ring she'd ever hoped to be given. "Although there wasn't a question, my answer, today and every day, is *yes*."

"Hand out, Doc," he whispered and plucked the ring from its velvet perch. "The next time we make love, I want you wearing this ring and nothing *but* this ring."

She giggled and held out her left hand. Wiggled her fingers when he didn't immediately slide it on. "Cale, you're killing me! Put it on. I said yes!"

He placed the ring on her finger so sweetly. So carefully. For a big man, he had the lightest, kindest touch. "You like it?" His eyes had misted, the emotion shimmering there sending affection, love, and lust right through her. Oh, how she adored this man. "We don't have to keep this one, if you don't."

"I love it. I love *you*." She tilted her hand back and forth, sending facets dancing across the pine planks. "I couldn't have picked a ring I'd cherish more."

"Truthfully, I wanted a stone the exact color your eyes turn when I'm deep inside you. When I found that, it was a done deal." A burst of red flowed into his cheeks. "Course, I didn't tell Elle that much."

"Sure of yourself, weren't you?"

He dropped his brow to hers and released a deep sigh that fluttered along the nape of her neck and straight into her heart. "No, Doc, I was only sure about *you*."

"You are my dream, Caleb Garrett." She cupped his cheeks and brought his lips to hers. "But I think you need a little persuading."

So she spent the rest of the afternoon making sure he knew exactly how much she loved him.

Wearing the ring and nothing else.

Epilogue

Eighteen Months Later

MACY LET SAND FUNNEL THROUGH her cupped fist as Caleb waded from the ocean, his shirt translucent, his thin cotton breeches adhering to his body so intimately her heart faltered. His cheeks were sun-tinged, his hair a dusky mess tangled about his head. *Beautiful.*

Mine.

She handed him a towel when he reached her, watching as he mopped his face and chest. Hasty swipes over lean hips, muscular thighs. His gaze was heated when it found hers. "If you keep looking at me with those hot eyes, I'm going to make apologies to the family when they get here and find a quiet spot for us. They'll understand. The men will at least."

She sank into the dune, the glow of a southern summer day spreading through her. "Remember the time behind the copse of loblolly pines? At the spring festival?" She trailed her toe along the inside of his calf. "Later, I found sand in some very interesting places."

He dropped down beside her, covering the front

of his breeches with the towel. "You fight dirty,
Dr. Garrett. Little Mouse"—he gestured to her
gently rounded stomach—"is making you greedy.
Every night and most mornings. I can't believe I'm
saying this, but damn, woman, I'm exhausted."

She rolled against him, placed her lips atop his
and did exactly what she knew drove him wild.
The man liked fierce, combative kisses. "I want
to fight dirty," she breathed, her hand drifting
beneath the towel. With a groan of surrender, he
swung her into his arms and raced to the surf. The
waves crashed around his knees as he splashed his
way in, whipping her ankles and tugging at her
skirt. "Caleb Eli Garrett, I'm not dressed for this!
You requested I do no swimming in my delicate
condition."

"With me you're safe, love. Don't you know
that by now?" When the water passed his naval,
she began to understand his purpose. She turned
in his arms, locked her legs around his waist as
he raised her skirt. His shaft was long and hard,
pressing into her thigh, begging for entry. His
hands went to her bottom, a slight lift, tilt. When
they were joined, with one glorious, urgent surge,
he captured her lips in a caress she felt to her core.

"You're the love of my life," she whispered
against the soft skin beneath his jaw. "Some days,
I'm still stunned. I thought medicine was all I was
ever going to have."

He halted, holding her steady and gazing into
her eyes. His were the warm, rich pewter of a
stormy sky. "I can do one better, Doc. You *are*

my life. You and little Mouse. I still don't think
I'm—"

"Hush. *You*, my artistic boatbuilder, are
everything."

When he only smiled and pulled her closer, she
felt certain he was beginning to believe her.

THE END

THANKS FOR READING *TIDES OF Desire*!
Curious about Zach and Savannah's sizzling
love story? Want to see how Noah charms the girl
he's always loved? Continue reading for a sneak
peek of *Tides of Passion* and *Tides of Love*. Feisty
Southern suffragettes in the Gilded Age!

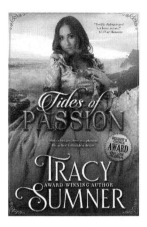

CHAPTER 1

Women can't have an honest exchange
in front of men without having it called a cat fight.
~Clare Boothe Luce

Outer Banks, NC
1898

SAVANNAH KNEW SHE WAS IN trouble a split second before he reached her.

Perhaps she should have saved herself the embarrassment of a tussle with the town constable, a man determined to believe the worst of her.

However, running from a challenge wasn't her way.

She laughed, appalled to realize it wasn't fear that had her contemplating slipping off the rickety crate and into the budding crowd gathered outside the oyster factory.

No, her distress was due to nothing more than Constable Garrett's lack of proper *clothing*.

In a manner typical of the coastal community she had temporarily settled in, his shirt lay open nearly to his *waist*. She couldn't help but watch the ragged shirttail flick his lean stomach as he advanced on her. Tall, broad-shouldered and lean-hipped, his physique belied his composed expression. Yet Savannah detected a faint edge of anger pulsing beneath the calm façade, one she wanted to deny sent her heart racing.

Wanted... but could not.

Flinging her fist into the air, she stared him down as she shouted, "Fight for your rights, women of Pilot Isle!"

The roar of the crowd, men in discord, women in glorious agreement, eclipsed her next call to action. *There*, she thought, pleased to see Zachariah Garrett's long-lashed gray eyes narrow, his golden skin pulling tight in a frown. Again she shook her fist, and the crowd bellowed.

One man ripped the sign Savannah had hung from the warehouse wall to pieces and fed it to the flames shooting from a nearby barrel. Another began channeling the group of protesting women away from the entrance. Many looked at her with proud smiles on their faces or raised a hand as they passed. They felt the pulse thrumming through the air, the energy.

There was no power like the power of a crowd.

Standing on a wobbly crate on a dock alongside the ocean, Savannah let the madness rush over her, sure, completely sure to the depths of her soul, that *this* was worth her often forlorn existence. Change was good. Change was necessary. And while she was here, she would make sure Pilot Isle saw its fair share.

"That's it for the show, Miss Connor," Zachariah Garrett said, wrapping his arm around her waist and yanking her from the crate as people swarmed past. "You've done nothing but cause trouble since you got here, and personally, I've about had it."

"I'm sorry, Constable, but that's the purpose of my profession!"

He set her on her feet none too gently and whispered in her ear, "Not in my town it isn't."

As she prepared to argue—Savannah was *always* prepared to argue—a violent shove forced her to her knees. Sucking in a painful gasp, she scrambled between the constable's long legs and behind a water cask. Dropping to a sit, she brushed a bead of perspiration from her brow and wondered what the inside of Pilot Isle's jail was going to look like.

Fatigue returned, along with the first flicker of doubt she had experienced in many a month. Resting her cheek on her knee, she let the sound of waves slapping the wharf calm her, the fierce breeze rolling off the sea cool her skin. Her family had lived on the coast for a summer when she was a child. It was one of the last times she remembered being truly happy.

Or loved.

Blessed God, how long ago that seemed now.

That was how Zach found her. Crouched behind a stinking fish barrel, dark hair a sodden mess hanging down her back, her dress—one that cost a pretty penny, he would bet—ripped and stained. She looked young at that moment, younger than he knew her to be. And harmless.

Which was as far from the truth as it got.

He shoved aside the sympathetic twinge, determined not to let his role as a father cloud every damned judgment he made. Due to this woman's meddling, his town folk pulsed like an angry wound behind him, the ringing of the ferry bell not doing a blessed thing to quiet a soul. All he could do was stare at the instigator huddling on a section of grimy planks and question how one uppity woman could stir people up like she'd taken a stick to their rear ends.

No wonder she was a successful social reformer up north. She was as good at causing trouble as any person he'd ever seen.

"Get up," Zach said, nudging her ankle with his boot. A slim, delicate-looking ankle.

He didn't like her, this sassy, liberating *rabble-rouser*, but he was a man, and he had to admit she was put together nicely.

She lifted her head, blinking, seeming to pull herself from a distant place. A halo of shiny curls brushed her jaw, and as she tilted her head up, he got his first close look at her. A fine-boned face, the expression on it soft, almost dreamy.

Boy, the softness didn't last long.

Jamming her lips together, her cheeks plumped with a frown. Oh yeah, that was the look he'd been expecting.

"Good day, Constable," she said. Just like that, as if he should be offering a cordial greeting with a small war going on behind them.

"Miss Connor, this way if you please."

She rose with all the dignity of a queen, shook out her skirts, and brushed dirt from one sleeve. He counted to ten and back, unruffled, good at hiding his impatience. What being the lone parent of a rambunctious little boy would do for a man.

Just when he reached ten for the second time and opened his mouth to order her along, a misplaced swing caught him in the side and he stumbled forward, grasping Savannah's shoulders to keep from crashing into her. Motion ceased when she thumped the wall of the warehouse, her head coming up fast, her eyes wide and alarmed.

And very, very green.

He felt the heat of her skin through the thin material of her dress; her muscles jumped beneath his palms. Her gaze dropped to his chest, and a soft glow lit her cheeks. Blushing... something he wouldn't have expected from *this* woman.

Nevertheless, he stared, wondering why they both seemed frozen.

Zach was frozen because he'd forgotten what it felt like to touch a woman. How soft and round and warm they were. How they dabbed perfume in secret places and smiled teasing smiles and flicked those colorful little fans in your face, never *really* realizing what all that nonsense did to a man's equilibrium.

It was the first time he'd laid his hands on a woman since his wife died, except for a rescue last year and the captain's sister he'd pulled from the sea. *She* had thrown her arms around him, shivering and crying, and he'd felt for her, sure he had. Grateful and relieved and humble that God had once again shown him where the lost souls on the shoals were.

He hadn't felt anything more. Anything strong.

This wasn't strong either, nothing more than a minute spike of heat in his belly.

Nothing much at all. He didn't *need* like other men. Like his brothers or his friends in town. He had needed once, needed his *wife*. But she was dead. That life—loving and yearning and wanting—had died with her.

"Your mouth is bleeding," Savannah said and shifted, her arm rising.

Don't touch me, he thought, the words bubbling in his throat.

Cursing beneath his breath, the full extent of his childishness struck him. She would think he'd gone crazy. And maybe he had. Stepping back, he thrust his hands in his pockets and gestured for her to follow, intentionally leading her away from the ruckus on the wharf.

Buttoning his shirt, he listened to her steady footfalls, thinking she'd be safe in his office until everything died down.

"I'm sorry you've been injured."

Dabbing at the corner of his lip, he shrugged. He could still hear the rumble of the crowd. No matter. His brother Caleb would break it up. They'd argued about who got what job in this mess.

Zach had lost.

"What did you expect, Miss Connor?" he finally asked. "People get heated, and they do stupid things like fight with their neighbors and their friends. Hard not to get vexed with you standing up there, rising from the mist, preaching and persuading, stirring emotion like a witch with a cauldron."

She rushed to catch up to him, and he slowed his deliberately forceful stride. "Those women work twelve-hour days, Constable Garrett. Twelve hours on their feet, often without lunch breaks or access to sanitary drinking water. And for half the pay a man receives for the same day's work. Some are expecting a child and alone, young women who think they can disappear in this town without their families ever finding them. Their lives up to this point have been so dominated and environed by duties, so largely ordered for them, that many don't know how to balance a cash account of modest means or find work of any kind that doesn't involve sewing a straight stitch or shucking oysters."

She stomped around a puddle in their path, kicking at shells and muttering, nicking her polished boots in the process. "If you can reconcile that treatment to your sense of what is just, then we have nothing more to discuss."

Zach halted before the unpretentious building that housed Pilot Isle's lone jail cell, getting riled himself, an emotion he rarely tolerated. He didn't know whether he should apologize or shake the stuffing out of her. "I'll be glad to tell you what I reconcile on a given day: business disputes, marriages, deaths, shipwrecks, the resulting cargo and bodies that wash up on shore, and just about everything in between. What you're talking about over at the oyster factory has been going on forever. Long hours, dreadfully long. The men may well get paid a higher wage—I couldn't say for certain—but they labor like mules, too. Do you think Hyman Carter is begging people to come work for him? Well, he isn't. It's a choice, free and clear." Reaching around her and flinging the door open, he stepped inside and, by God, expected her to follow. "What the hell can I do about that?"

Her abrupt silence had him turning. Savannah Connor stood in the doorway, bright sunlight flooding in around her, again looking like a vision of blamelessness, of sweet charity. She even smiled, closing the door gently behind her. Troubled, Zach reviewed his last words, racing through them in his mind.

"Oh no," he said, flinging his hand up in a motion his son knew meant no, flat out. "I'm not getting involved in this campaign of yours. Except to end it, I'm not getting involved."

"Why not get involved?" she asked, the edge

back. "Give me one worthy reason why. You're the perfect person to request a review of the factory's processes."

Ignoring her, he slumped into the chair behind his desk, dug his cargo ledger out of the top drawer and a water-stained list out of his pocket, and began calculating entries. He was two shipwrecks behind. The town couldn't auction property—funds they desperately needed—until he, as keeper of Life-saving Division Six, completed the sad task of recording every damaged plank, every broken teacup, every sailor's shoe.

Work was good for the soul, he had always thought; it had saved *his* a couple of years ago.

Besides, maybe Miss Connor would quit talking if he didn't look at her.

Moments passed, the only sound the scratch of pen across paper and the occasional crunch of wagon wheels over the shell-paved street out front. When the cell's metal door squealed, Zach started, flicking ink across the page. He sighed. "I'm almost afraid to ask what you're doing."

Looking up from plumping the cot's pillow, she flashed a tight smile. "Getting ready for a long night, Constable Garrett. You're writing"—she pointed—"a summons for me in that little book, correct? What will it be? Disturbing the peace? Instigating a mutiny?" She shrugged, clearly unconcerned. "I've been charged with both of those before."

The fountain pen dropped from Zach's fingers. "*Arrested*? Ma'am, I've no intention of—"

"Thirteen if you count the incident in Baltimore. That time, the police took us to a school instead of the local station. They didn't have a separate holding area for women and felt it would be inappropriate for my group to share quarters with common offenders."

Thirteen. Zach coughed to clear his throat. "I'm not arresting you. I only brought you here until things calm down on the wharf."

Savannah smiled, relief evident in the droop of her shoulders. "Then you'll help me. Thank goodness."

Gripping the desk, he shoved back his chair. "No way, no how. Are you deaf, ma'am?"

"Are *you*, sir? Did you hear those women out there today begging for equal rights? Women under your protection I might add."

His lids slipped low, the spasm of pain in his chest hitting him hard. *Protect.* Zach had spent his life trying to protect people. And so far he'd failed his wife, his brothers, and 81 passengers that he and his men had not gotten to in time. All events Reverend Tiernan said were in God's hands and God's hands only.

On good days, Zach agreed.

Opening his eyes, he forced his way back to his work, recording the wrong number in the wrong column. "Hyman Carter is a decent man. Pays his taxes, attends town meetings. He even donated enough money for the church to buy new pews last spring."

"He bought your loyalty in exchange for pews?"

His head snapped up. "No one buys my *anything*, Miss Connor."

She simply raised a perfectly shaped brow, sending his temper soaring two notches.

"Listen here, ma'am. That scene you caused today isn't the way to accomplish much in a town like this, though I'm sure it works fine in New York City. Personally, I don't cotton to taking orders from a mulish suffragette whose only aim in life is to secure the vote."

She took a fast step forward, her cheeks pinking. "Constable Garrett, you've grown too comfortable."

"That I have."

"No excuses?"

"Not a one."

"Well, you must know I won't rest until we come to a reasonable compromise."

"All right, then, you must know I can't change a man's way of running his business if it doesn't fall outside the law." He dipped his head in a mock show of respect. "Ma'am."

"Don't you realize that the situation at the oyster factory isn't *just*?"

A headache he hadn't felt coming roared to life. Pressing his fingers to his temple, Zach said, weary and unrepentant, "When did you get the idea life was just, Miss Connor?"

Savannah turned, pacing the length of the small cell, the sudden flicker of emotion in Zachariah Garrett's smoke-gray eyes more than she wanted to see, more than she could allow herself to.

Feeling sympathy for an opponent violated a basic tenet of the abolitionist code. And whether she liked it or not, this man was the gatekeeper.

In more ways than one. She'd only been in town a week, but it was easy to see who people in Pilot Isle turned to in crisis. She had heard his name a thousand times already.

Just when she had devised a skillful argument to present for his inspection, a much better one strolled through the office door.

The woman was attractive and trim... and quite obviously smitten with Constable Garrett. Unbeknownst to him, she smoothed her hand the length of her bodice and straightened the straw hat atop her head before making her presence known.

"Gracious, Zach, *what* is going on in town today?"

Zach slowly lifted his head, shooting a frigid glare Savannah's way before pasting a smile on his face and swiveling around on his stubborn rump. "Miss Lydia, I hope you didn't get caught up in that mess. Caleb should have it under control by now though."

Miss Lydia drifted toward the desk, her clear blue gaze focused so intently on the man behind it that Savannah feared the woman would trip over her own feet if she wasn't careful. "Oh, I didn't get near it, you know that would never do. If Papa heard, he'd have a conniption. But I *was* at Mr. Scoggin's store and it was all anyone could talk about." She placed a cloth- covered basket on his desk. The scent of cinnamon filled the room.

"Lands, imagine the excitement of a rally, right here in Pilot Isle."

Zach sighed. "Yes, imagine that."

"And"—Lydia glanced in her direction—"you've, um, detained *her.*"

"I haven't—"

"Constable Garrett, if I may?" Savannah gestured to the cell door she'd shut while Miss Lydia stood in the threshold, hand-pressing her bodice. "I promise to be on my best behavior. It's just so hard to converse through metal bars."

"Oh, dear Lord." Zach yanked a drawer open and fished for a set of keys he clearly didn't use often. Stalking toward the cell with murder in his eyes, he asked in a low tone, "What game are you playing, Miss Connor?"

"Forewarned is forearmed, Constable."

With a snap of his wrist and a compelling shift of muscle beneath the sleeve of his shirt, he opened the door. "*Out.*"

"My, my, Constable, such hospitality for a humble inmate." She plucked her skirt between her fingers and circled him as she imagined a belle of the ball would.

Belle of the ball was called for with Miss Lydia, Savannah had realized from the first moment. The bored woman of consequence needing fulfillment.

And a cause.

Savannah would gladly give her one.

"If I may introduce myself." Savannah halted before Miss Lydia and flashed a hesitant smile.

"Savannah Connor. Pleased to make your acquaintance."

Miss Lydia struggled for a moment but good breeding won out. In the South, it always seemed to. "Lydia Alice Templeton. Pleased, also, I'm sure." She gestured to the basket on the desk. "Would you like a muffin? You must be starved, poor thing. These are my special recipe. Cinnamon and brown sugar, and a secret ingredient I won't tell to save my life. Zach, oh." She tapped her bottom lip with a gloved finger. "Mr. Garrett, loves them."

"I'm sure he does," Savannah said, not having to turn to see his displeasure. It radiated, like a hot brand pressed to her back. "And I would love one. I'm practically faint with hunger."

Miss Lydia sprang into action, unfastening and cutting, spreading butter, and clucking like a mother hen. Savannah admired women who could nurture like that; Miss Lydia was a born mother when children scared Savannah half to death.

"Here, dear," Miss Lydia murmured, full of warmth and compassion. "Mr. Garrett, haven't you a pitcher of water?"

No reply, but within a minute a chipped jug and a glass appeared on the desk with a brusque clatter.

"Do you mind if I perch right here on the corner of your desk, Constable?" Savannah asked and bit into the most delicious muffin she had ever tasted. "Truly, these *are* good. Ummm."

"I win the blue ribbon every year at the Harvest Celebration." Lydia shrugged as if this were a certain thing in her life. "My father owns a commercial fishing company, and my mother passed some time ago, so I take care of him now. I bake all day some days." She turned her hand in a dreamy circle. "To fill the time."

Savannah halted, a mouthful of muffin resting on her tongue. She couldn't stop herself—really, the urge was too powerful—from looking up. Constable Garrett stood in the cell's entryway, shoulder jammed against a metal bar, feet crossed at the ankle, those startling gray eyes trained on her. Trained without apology.

"*No*," he mouthed. An honest appeal from an honest man.

She hadn't dealt with many honest men in her life, including her father and her brother. Also, she was confident she hadn't ever had as attractive an opponent. It was wicked to feel a tiny zing when she imagined besting him, wasn't it? Was that letting personal issues and professional ones collide?

Swallowing, she returned her attention to her prey. "You could find other ways to fill your time. I'm happy to tell you that this is precisely what I did."

"But—"

"My mother also passed away when I was a young girl. After that my life consisted of living in our home in New York City, while making a life for my father and my older brother. They were helpless when it came to running a household, so I took over. My childhood ended at that time, but later on, I made sure I would have something to show for it."

"Ohhh," Lydia said, clasping her hand to her heart.

Savannah ignored the audible grunt from the back of the room and continued, "One day I simply found the endless duties and tasks, many of which I was uninterested in, to be so monotonous as to make my life seem worthless. I forced myself to search for meaning—a cause, if you will. I attended my first women's rights meeting the next afternoon." She failed to mention she had been all of sixteen and had nearly broken her ankle jumping from the window of her bedroom to the closest tree limb outside. After dragging her home from the meeting, her father had locked her in her bedroom for two days.

Without food or water.

He didn't let her out until that lovely old tree outside her window no longer stood tall and proud.

"Miss Connor, I couldn't possibly attend a meeting like that here."

Savannah dabbed a muffin crumb from the desk and licked her finger. "Why ever not?"

"It's not... I'm not...." Lydia's voice trailed off.

"You're not resilient enough? Oh, you are. I could tell right away. Can you honestly say that you are satisfied with your life? What, pray tell, are you doing completely for yourself?"

"Redecorating my father's stu—"

"That's for him. Try again."

"Cooking."

Savannah smiled and shook her head.

Lydia snapped her fingers. "Oh, I have one! I host an information-gathering tea in the historical society office one morning a week. Although Papa feels it's shameful for me to work, even when the position is entirely without compensation."

Savannah relaxed her shoulders, dabbed at another crumb, as if the news weren't simply wonderful. The glow of heat at her back seemed to increase. "And how do you feel about working?"

"I love it. I'm very good at keeping records and tallying donations. I raised more money for the society last year than any other volunteer, even though Sallie Rutherford's total arrived at five dollars more than mine." She leaned in, cupping her hand around her mouth. "Hyman Carter is her uncle, and he gave it to her at the last minute to lift her total past mine."

The wonder, Savannah thought, dizzy with promise. "Miss Templeton, this is a propitious conversation. I need a co-leader for my efforts and until this moment, I wasn't sure I would be able to locate the right woman in a town the size of Pilot Isle." She smiled, placing her hand over Lydia's gloved fingers. "Now, I think I have."

"Me?" Lydia breathed, hand climbing to her chest. "A co-leader?"

Savannah nodded. "I have to govern Elle Beaumont's school in her absence. Teach classes and mentor her female students until her return. You may have heard that she's returned to university in South Carolina. Yet, I couldn't possibly stay here and watch women live in a state of disability and not try to improve their situation. Women working exhausting hours for half the pay a man receives, for instance. Did you know about that?"

"The oyster factory? Well, I have to say, that is, yes." Her gaze skipped to the constable and back. "Although, I haven't ever been employed. Not in a true position of payment. And the factory," she said, voice dropping to a whisper, "isn't where any ladies of, what did you call it, *consequence* are likely to pay a visit."

"As co-leader of the Pilot Isle movement, you should make it your first stop. Let's plan to meet there tomorrow morning. Nine o'clock sharp. Bring Miss Rutherford, who even if she is a bit of a charlatan, might prove a worthy supporter. Too, she can gain access for the group without the burden of another impassioned assembly."

Savannah smiled and added, "Surely her uncle doesn't want that."

"Now wait a blessed minute."

Savannah glanced up as Zach's shadow flooded over them. Bits of dust drifted through the wide beam of sunlight he stood in, softening the intensity of his displeasure. No matter his inflexibility, the man was attractive.

"A problem, Constable?"

"You're damn right there's a problem."

A soft gasp had him bowing slightly and

frowning harder. "Beg pardon, Miss Lydia. I apologize for the language, but this doesn't concern you." He swung Savannah around on the desk, her knees banging his as he crouched before her, bringing their eyes level. "It concerns *you*, and I remember telling *you* I wasn't putting up with this foolishness." He stabbed his finger against his chest. "Not in my town."

She drew a covert breath. Traces of manual labor and the faintest scent of cinnamon circled him. Savannah valued hard work above all else and never minded a man who confirmed he valued it as well, even if he smelled less than soap-fresh and his palms were a bit rough. Forcing her mind to the issue at hand, she asked, "Are we prohibited from visiting the factory, Constable?"

"After today, you better believe you are."

She arched a brow, a trick she had practiced before the mirror for months until it alone exemplified frosty indifference. "My colleagues, Miss Templeton and Miss Rutherford, will attend in my absence, then."

"No."

She scooted forward until the stubble dotting his rigid jaw filled her vision. "You can't stop them and you know it. In fact, I'm fairly certain you cannot stop *me* without filing paperwork barring me from Mr. Carter's property. That takes time and signatures, rounding up witnesses to the dispute. However, I'm willing to forgo this meeting. During the initial phase at any rate. For everyone's comfort."

Sliding back the inch she needed to pull their knees apart, she decided that for all Zachariah Garrett's irritability—a trait she abhorred in a man—he smelled far, far too tempting to risk touching during negotiations. "Don't challenge my generosity, Mr. Garrett. You won't get more."

"Are you daring me to do something, Miss Connor? Because I will, I tell you."

"Consider it a gracious request."

"You can take your gracious request and stick it...." Jamming his hands atop his knees, he rose to his feet. "Miss Lydia, will you excuse us a moment?"

Lydia cleared her throat and backed up two steps. Before she left, she looked at Savannah and smiled, her eyes bright with excitement. Savannah returned the smile, knowing she had won that series if nothing else.

"You must be crazy," Zach said the moment the door closed. "Look at the blood on your dress, the scrapes on your hands. Do you want Miss Lydia to suffer the same? The things you want her to experience are things her father has purposely kept her from experiencing and for a damn good reason."

She gazed at the torn skin on her hands and the traces of blood on her skirt as she heard him begin to pace the narrow confines of the office. "It's a mockery to talk of sheltering women from life's fierce storms, Constable. Do you believe the ones who work twelve-hour days in that factory are too weak to weather the emotional stress of a political campaign? Do you believe Lydia cannot support a belief that runs counter to her father's? A child is not a replica of the parent. The sexes, excuse my frankness, do not have the same challenges in life."

Watching him, his hands buried in his pockets—to keep from circling her neck she supposed—she couldn't help but marvel at the curious mix of Southern courtesy and male arrogance, the natural assumption he shouldered of being lawfully in control. "Engaging in a moral battle isn't always hazardous to one's health, you know."

"Doesn't look like it's doing wonders for yours."

"Saints be praised, it can actually be *rewarding*."

Looking over his shoulder, he halted in the middle of the room. "Irish."

"I beg your pardon?"

"You. Irish. The green eyes, the tiny bit of red in your hair. Is Connor your real name?"

"Yes, why," she said, stammering. *Oh, hell.* "Of course."

"Liar."

She felt the slow, hot roll of color cross her cheeks. "What could that possibly have to do with anything?"

"I don't know, but I have a feeling it means something. It's the first thing I've heard come out of that sassy mouth of yours that didn't sound like some damned speech." He tapped his head, starting to pace again. "What I wonder is, where are *you* in there?"

"I'm right here. Reasonable and... and judicious.

Driven perhaps but not sassy, never sassy."

"You're full of piss and vinegar, all right. And some powerful determination to cause me problems when I have more than I can handle." He halted in the middle of the room. "And here I thought Ellie was difficult. Opening that woman's school and teaching God knows what in that shed behind Widow Wynne's, putting husbands and fathers in an uproar. Now you're here, and it's ten times worse than it ever was before."

"Do women have to roll over like a dog begging for a scratch for men to value them?"

"That and a pretty face work well enough for me."

She hopped to her feet, her skirt slapping the desk. "You insufferable toad."

"Better that than a reckless nuisance."

"There's nothing wrong with feeling passionate about freedom, Constable Garrett. And I plan to let every woman in this town know it."

"If it means causing the kind of scene you caused today, you'll have to go through me first."

Savannah laughed, wishing it hadn't come out sounding so much like a cackle. "I've heard that several hundred times in the past. With no result, I might add."

"Guess you have." Halting before a tall cabinet scarred in more places than not, he went up on the toes of his boots and came back with a bottle. Another reach earned a glass. "With thirteen detentions, I can't say I'm surprised." She watched him pour a precise measure, tilt his head, and throw it back. "Did any of them happen to figure out you were working Irish underneath the prissy clothes and snooty manners?"

She lowered her chin, quickly, before he could spotlight her distress. *Working Irish.* A term she hadn't heard in years. Every horrible trait she possessed—willfulness, callousness, condescension—her father said came from the dirty Irish blood flowing through her veins. Her mother had been the immigrant who had trapped him in an unhappy marriage.

A marriage beneath his station, thank you very much.

And he had never let his family forget it.

"Would you like a medal for your perspicacious deduction, Constable?" she asked when she'd regained her composure.

He laughed and saluted her with his glass. "Heck, I don't even know what that means."

"*Astute*, Constable. Which you are. Surprisingly so." She closed the distance between them and took the glass from his clenched fist, ignoring the warmth of his skin when their fingers touched.

"May I?" she asked and drained the rest, liquid fire burning its way down. Looking at him from beneath her lashes, she smiled. "The Irish like the taste of whiskey on their tongues, did you know that? O'Connor was my mother's maiden name. Her grandfather changed it to Connor when he came through Ellis Island. When my father asked me to vacate his home the first time, I claimed the name because he said if I must disgrace the family,

I could disgrace her side of it. So I did."

She handed the glass back. "Now that you know one of my secrets, I should know one of yours."

He went very still, the arm that held the bottle dropping to his side. Before he pivoted on his heel, his face revealed such wretched grief that she felt the pain like a dart through her own heart. It wasn't enough to offer an apology for the offense.

How could she when she wasn't sure what ground she had trespassed on?

"After she got released from jail, we had coffee she bought specially in New York City. About the best coffee I've ever tasted, too. And these hard, bready cookies that Savannah"—Lydia cupped her hand around her mouth—"I call her that now you know, said she has to go to a place called Little Italy in New York City to buy. Can you imagine? And I'm to be her co-leader. My goodness, I never would have thought anything this exciting would happen in Pilot Isle. Not in my lifetime."

"Your father?" Sallie Rutherford asked in a hushed whisper, pleating her skirt with shaky fingers.

"Oh, he'll shoot me dead when he finds out." Lydia fanned her warm cheeks, trying hard not to envision her father's certain fit of temper. "But I'm strong enough to handle him. Resilient, yes."

"And you're still planning to go tomorrow morning?"

She nodded. "With you."

"Oh dear me, no. Dwight looks like he's sucking a lemon most days as it is. Do you want him to move back to his mother's for *good*?" Dwight Rutherford had married Sallie Smithe on the eve of his fortieth birthday and any disturbance on the calm sea of life sent him running back to his boyhood home and the welcoming arms of his mother.

"Savannah said there's nothing wrong with helping your fellow woman, Sallie. Why should we expect the men in this town to be happy about it, can you tell me that? It's a man's world; laws are men's laws; the government a man's government. We're merely set on changing that."

Lydia felt sure Savannah would have been pleased to hear her parroting with such accuracy.

"Well, what about Dwight? And your father?"

"Oh, posh." Lydia chewed the last of her iced fruitcake with renewed enthusiasm. "They can take a big old leap off Pearson's dock for all I care."

"But the quilting meeting is—"

"Hang Nora and her weekly quilting meeting! I need you to get past the men your uncle will undoubtedly have guarding the gate. Plus, he won't curse too much with you in the room." Lydia dipped her linen napkin in a finger bowl on the table and patted the cool cloth against her lips. She ignored the beads of perspiration rolling down her back. Insufferable summers. "After the historical society calamity last year, you *owe* me. How can you even consider refusing?"

"Why, I never," Sallie sputtered with all the

indignation of an affronted peacock.

Lydia drew a deep breath, testing the air to see if the roast she was cooking for dinner needed checking. "Savannah's going to unpack the rest of her belongings today. Books, pamphlets, materials to make signs. Paint and paper, all the way from New York. She also has badges for us to wear. Red with the words Freedom Fighter in gold emblazed across it."

"Gold?"

"If you help us with this, you'll be a bona fide member of the Pilot Isle Ladies Freedom Fighters."

"My...." Sallie sank back against the plump cushions, a wistful look entering her eyes.

Lydia released a pent-up sigh, less frightened than good sense should allow she knew. Savannah and the rally and the chance to live life for herself just this once was too rare an opportunity to let slip away. Besides, Zach Garrett wouldn't let them dilly-dally for more than a day or two.

She needed to have her amusement now.

"I'll do it," Sallie surprised her by saying, quite clearly and without additional arm-twisting.

Lydia clapped her hands and giggled, giddy to the tips of her patent leather boots. "That is fine news. I'm thrilled and relieved. Gracious, now that that's settled, I must tell you what else happened at the jail. I shouldn't, but I simply must."

Sallie vaulted to a rigid position, eager for gossip.

"I really shouldn't say—"

"Oh no, please do! It's been so dull around here since Noah Garrett ran off with that crazy Elle

Beaumont."

Too true, Lydia thought. The entire town had hungrily monitored the antics of Zach's youngest brother and Elle Beaumont, who, eccentric as she seemed to be, had snared the man she'd wanted since long before anyone could remember differently. It made her think of... well, today, at the jail, the way Zach had looked at Savannah, just for a hint of a moment when he thought no one was looking.

Not with interest, no, no, *no*. More as though he had been wound up like one of those new-fangled toys she'd seen in the window of Dillon's Goods in Raleigh.

Agitated was a good word for it. Which was all well and fine because women often roused men to a fever pitch.

Everyone knew that. It was just the way life operated.

Except it never seemed to operate like that for Zachariah Garrett. Even when his beloved wife was alive, he'd been calm and capable and strong. Why, if Lydia felt half a heart in love with him it was *because* she'd never witnessed anything but calm, capable, strong Constable Garrett.

She had never seen him agitated. *Never.*

Lydia wouldn't have guessed he had it in him.

Maybe there was something to this independence craze if it made a man sit up and take notice.

"Of course, this cannot go any further than this parlor," she finally said, tucking a wisp of damp hair beneath her bonnet. "And again, I shouldn't say, but I have to tell you that I've never seen such fire in Constable Garrett's eyes as I did today."

"*Fire*? Zach Garrett?" Sallie swallowed a bite of iced fruitcake too quickly and choked. "Are... are you sure? Why, he's so *collected*."

"Without a doubt. Fire," Lydia assured her friend. "And Savannah Connor lit the match."

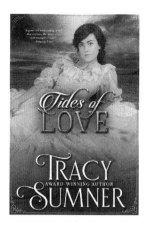

CHAPTER 1

"The first plan is the simplest
and the one most usually adopted."
C. Wyville Thomson
The Depths of the Sea

1898, Chicago

NOAH MARKED FOUR NOTCHES IN the top of the ship's keel and pushed up his shirtsleeves, rechecking his measurements. He was adding the figures in his head faster than he could with paper and pencil when a knock sounded on the door.

"Coming," he muttered beneath his breath, but didn't rise. He disliked finishing a model section and leaving his materials spread over his desk.

"Garrett, I know you're in there." The door rattled on its tracks, yanked from the outside.

Noah groaned and stretched, crossed the room and let Bryant Bigelow, the ruddy-checked fisheries commissioner, charge inside.

"Dammit, Garrett. Freezing in that hallway." Bigelow blew into his hands and stamped his feet. His sodden pilot coat fluttered at his ankles, nearly brushing the floor. The former Navy captain, all bluster and brashness, stood just over five feet tall. "Christ Almighty. Freezing in here, too."

"Is it?" Noah grabbed a sweater from a rusty hook and tugged it past his head. He smoothed the scratchy wool, let his palm linger over his twitching stomach muscles. He pressed hard, sucking in a furtive breath. *Maintain a calm facade,* he ordered himself.

"Why in God's name do you live here? Never felt a colder place in my life." Bigelow advanced into the center of the enormous chamber, loosening a crimson scarf from his throat. "All this junk. Shells and"—he jabbed his boot against a rusted anchor—"ship models. And books. How many you have here, Garrett? A hundred? A thousand?" He angled his head, fixing his flinty gaze on Noah. His fleshy lips twisted in what he probably considered a smile. "You're the finest biologist I've ever worked with, but sometimes I think you're crazy."

The jarring squeal of the Union Loop Elevated kept Noah from having to reply. At first, he'd hated the metallic, ceaseless screeching on the tracks below. Now, he found sleep difficult without the train rattling the glass panes. Of course, he could live in Jackson Park with the other biologists or on Prairie Avenue with the educated elite. Admittedly, the space was impossible to heat during a typical Chicago winter. However, he could not, *would not*, explain his choice to distance himself from his colleagues.

Accounting for his idiosyncrasies made him decidedly uneasy.

"We have a problem, Garrett."

The blurred edges of Bigelow's face finally registered. Noah reached for his spectacles. "I would offer tea or coffee, as you look like a drowned rat but"—he slipped them on, blinked—"no facilities."

"You can't even boil a cup of water in this joint?"

"Afraid not." He shoved his hands deep in his trouser pockets, stiffening his shoulders, hoping the stance looked properly composed. He wasn't going to ask. Did not want to know.

Unfortunately, the rumors had made their way to his cramped office yesterday afternoon. He had been hiding in here ever since.

"I received another telegraph regarding the lab in North Carolina. Seems they prefer to work with a local. Soothe ruffled feathers of the fishermen or some such guff. You're from North Carolina, right?"

Circling toward the window, Noah squeezed his eyes shut. The sheer irony of life never ceased to amaze him.

Bigelow's leather soles cracked as he crossed the room, paused to fiddle with a row of horse conchs resting on a low shelf. "Anyway, we're ready to build. Need someone to supervise construction. You're the closest we have to a local, and you're the only man I have on staff who worked on the lab at Woods Hole. Our funding agreement contains conditions. Unfortunately, you've become one of them."

Noah watched a streetcar turn onto Dearborn Street, blue sparks spitting in its wake. "Last week, I received word a stipend has been approved for the trout acclimatization west of the Mississippi. I wanted to start working—"

"Give it to Thomas or someone on your crew. How many trout can one man save? Do you remember the disaster at Woods Hole? Didn't we learn our lesson?"

Noah heard a match strike, then Bigelow sucking on one of those foul cigars he loved. "You've been pushing for a second lab, Garrett. Well, here she is. A month or two living a stone's throw from some of the best barrier islands in the world doesn't sound terrible to me. Look at it this way, you can get research done, and you won't have to sleep or eat. Same as here, only warmer. Pilot Isle is perfect for you. No telephones. Hell, no electricity." He grunted, blew a noisy breath into the air. "I have to admit, this dawdling makes me question your commitment, son."

Noah shivered as ten years of grief and uncertainty, of raw, gut-wrenching fear, descended on his shoulders. *Commitment.* He would do anything to make the laboratory a success, was, in fact, the most devoted member of the fisheries department.

And Bryant Bigelow knew it.

"When do I leave?" he asked without turning, not wishing to record the victorious light in the commissioner's gaze or reveal the dread in his own.

"Soon as you're ready, Garrett. Soon, better be. Already leveling the foundation." He ground his heel to the floor, his smoking cigar stub no doubt beneath it.

Noah dipped his head, gripped the sill with both hands. A gust of wind off the lake rattled the windowpane in its frame, sent a frigid draft of air across his cheek.

After all the years of running, the past had finally caught him.

Noah had once believed nothing less than a decree from God would make him return to Pilot Isle.

Long ago, he'd convinced himself of his ability to live without his family, without Elle. Yet here he sat, bouncing across white-capped swells in a sturdy skiff clearly bearing the markings of his brother's design.

"You staying for the heated term, yup?"

Noah glanced over his shoulder. The old man sat at the stern of the boat, tiller in one hand, bottle of spirits in the other. He remembered the face, brown and withered, the pale scar splitting one cheek. He remembered the name, too—Stymie Hawkins. "You're pinching," he said without thinking, then frowned and turned toward the bow, wishing he had kept his damn mouth shut.

"Pinching?" The skiff rocked with Stymie's abrupt movement. A dry cough, then a slurp that sounded like a swig from the bottle. "I reckon I can get us to the Isle, young fella."

Noah squinted and swabbed at his eyes. The spray of salty water had made it necessary to pocket his spectacles, but he could see well enough. Too well, perhaps. They were three hundred yards from docking, sailing past a ship anchored close to the wharf.

"Ready about." Stymie swung the boat into the wind. "Little storm brewing, bit of rain. No nor'easter... nothing like that. Hope you have a place to stay. Lodgings, what little we got, all crammed tight with gosh darned whalers."

"I made the necessary arrangements," Noah said, watching a row of peaked cypress roofs burst into view, upper porches rising above wind-shaped oaks. He grasped the sides of the skiff, the reality of returning stabbing deep, the urge to flee hitting hard.

Stymie altered course, thudding the pockmarked pier as he angled in. "Only one fella ever told me how to sail."

Startled, Noah straightened to his full height, an action he avoided with much shorter men. The breeze took advantage and ripped his coat wide. "Excuse me?"

Stymie released a whistle-breath through the gaping space in his teeth. "Professor used to tell me how to manage my sail. Pert near right most times. I think I mighta been pinching at that."

"Nice story." Noah shoved a few coins into Stymie's hand and took off down the pier.

The first raindrop smacked his face as he crossed the wharf, shrieking seagulls and pounding waves a seductively familiar chorus. He shouldered past a throng of whalers, cast-iron try pots slung across their shoulders, their ribald laughter peppering the air. He skirted a fishmonger's wagon and stepped over a length of rope. An old man perched on an overturned water cask glanced at him, lifted a weathered hand in greeting. Noah returned the gesture reluctantly and turned behind a concealing wall of stacked oyster barrels.

Humid air arrived in gusts from the east, thick from the increasingly steady drizzle, the final nod to the question of whether to wear his spectacles. *Maybe it's better,* he reasoned, pausing in front of a house facing the bay, the double porch sagging above a foundation of ballast stone, the cypress shake roof dull gray. The enticing scent of the marsh on the far side of the island distressed him enough without clear vision bringing added misery, transporting him back to a time of security and love, family and friendship. While he stood there, trying to remember whose house this had been, the loneliness inside him awakened, overflowing his heart, forcing aside every other emotion. Eyes downcast and shoulders hunched, he traversed the shell-paved lane, the owner of the house forgotten.

Shaking rain from his face, he broke into a trot. He must remember the promise he had made as his train exited Dearborn Station: he would not be drawn into wondering *what if;* drawn into reliving a period of his life he wished to forget; drawn into lowering his guard, allowing the people who had once meant the entire world to him to mean the world again. He had learned to survive on his own, after years of agonizing exertion.

No one to trust or lose trust in.

No one to risk his heart over.

By the time he arrived at Widow Wynne's boardinghouse, he had regained his equilibrium but lost most of his body heat. His wool underdrawers stuck to his skin, water dripped off his nose and slid past his collar. Cursing beneath his breath, he made a mad dash for the front porch and a reprieve from the storm.

The woman stepped into his path—or he stepped into hers. Her head bounced off his chest, his satchel landed in a puddle. His arms rose to steady her. "Excuse me, ma'am, terribly...." His voice tapered off.

Deep green eyes met his, glistening drops of water spiking the long lashes. A fierce ache started deep in his chest and moved to his gut.

Only one person had eyes as beautiful as these.

Goddamn luck, he thought.

Elle tipped her head, rain washing over her fading smile. She flicked a glance at the hands holding her. *"Juste Ciel,"* she said, her throat doing a slow draw as she swallowed. Her face paled, and she lifted a trembling hand to her forehead.

Noah braced his knees, fingers tightening around her slim forearms. For a moment, he feared she would pitch into the mud at their feet. But she simply mouthed his name as her gaze again fell to his hands.

Remembering she had always liked them, even impulsively called them beautiful once, he snatched them from her and searched blindly for his satchel, trying to escape the ringing in his ears, the darkness dimming his vision. Coming home had been a mistake. If it hurt this much to face Elle Beaumont, how would it feel to face his brothers?

"Wait. Noah, there's nowhere else to stay. Unless you want to go home."

He halted by the gate, threw his head back on his shoulders, and blinked the ashen sky into view. *Go home?* God, no. Water trickled in his mouth as he said, "Nowhere? There must be."

"I've already refused two fishermen. Widow Wynne returns from her niece's in a month. Then she'll accept boarders. Trust me, I would tell you if there were anywhere else."

Trust her? Oh, yes, *that* had turned out well before. Sighing, he cut his gaze her way, to find her standing in a shallow puddle, a sack of vegetables hanging forgotten from her fingers. A mannish blouse clung, somewhat indecently, to her bosom.

She had curves in places once flat and uninspiring.

So he stood there a moment, drenched and shivering, wondering how much better she would look if he had his spectacles on. "I could telephone—"

"No telephone. I petitioned the town committee for a public one, like they have in Morehead City. I proposed we place it at the mercantile." Swishing her toe through the puddle, she needlessly splashed her jersey gaiters with mud. "Mr. Scoggins planned to install it on the boardwalk post so his mother didn't have to see it. She threatened to move off the island if he did. Thinks spooks will creep along the line and into the store." She lifted her gaze, a mix of emotions crossing her face. Delight, caution, even a hint of anger, damn her. He read them all, like ink stamped on her forehead, the same as he could when they were children.

"We have a telegraph," she finally added.

"Impressive changes. There was a telegraph *before*."

"Yes, well"—he observed in amazement as she pulled a watch from a narrow slit in her skirt and flicked open the tarnished copper cover— "impressive or no, the office closed forty-five minutes ago." She blinked rain from her eyes and pocketed the watch, faltering when she caught his look. "Oh. I have the seamstress specially sew the pockets." She stamped her foot, splashing more muddy water on herself. "Why should a man be the only—"

For the love of God. "A hotel?"

She shoved a sodden clump of hair behind her ear, the ends bright against her skin. "You think we've gone this long without telephones but suddenly have hotels?"

A fat raindrop hit his neck and slipped inside his collar, making him shiver. He wasn't about to stand around in a downpour and explore his limited options. "Tell me this isn't your home, Elle."

She lifted her chin, a flush sweeping her cheeks.

"Tell me you're married and have three children. Tell me you're only bringing the widow her groceries."

She shook her head, an angry circle of white rimming her mouth.

No way, not living in the same goddamn *house,* he vowed, and kicked the gate open. Elle emitted a squeak of panic and caught him by the wrist, throwing him off-balance and against the white pickets rising between them. Her breasts, firm and plump, bumped his chest, and he recoiled, but not much. She had a remarkably strong grip for a petite woman, and perhaps, if he were honest, he didn't want to move badly enough.

"Don't. Please don't. Not again."

Grief and remorse claimed him. "You don't have any idea what it has taken to *get* me here. But you have an idea what it took to make me leave, don't you?" He raised his hand in apology. "I've agonized for two months about this. I waited until

I could... until I felt sure I could...." He tilted his head, icy drops of rain stinging his face.

"You're the marine biologist we've been expecting? The one I'm holding the coach house for?"

Nodding, he blew out a breath.

"I'll leave it to you to tell your brothers. I won't say a word. I promise. Caleb is gone for two more days, buying lumber in Durham. And Zach, well, Zach is here."

Noah closed his eyes, his skin prickling in anticipation and dread. Caleb and Zach. God, how he had missed them. "Too late for promises, Elle. Stymie Hawkins recognized me."

"Stymie Hawkins." She worried her bottom lip between her teeth. "It *will* be all over town by tomorrow then."

He tugged his hand through his hair. If he had a moment alone, he felt sure he could ease his discomfort. At least make a list of reasons for his return to Pilot Isle, something tangible to assess.

"Come in. Out of the rain," she said. "The coach house is very private. You have the second floor all to yourself."

A gust of wind pressed damp cotton against his chest, and he struggled to suppress a shudder.

"Some boxes arrived for you yesterday. Rory and I stacked them in the front room. Everything's clean, just a little dusty."

Who the hell is Rory, Noah wanted to ask? Her fiancé, most likely. *Good.* "Second floor?" he asked instead.

"It has a private entrance. Widow Wynne even had facilities installed last year."

"Facilities. Ye gods." Concentrating on the clank and rub of boats edging the dock and the bang of the unlatched gate against its post, he made an indecisive halt, a half turn. "I don't know, that is... I don't know if I can stay."

"I understand."

She probably did. Elle had always been able to sense his moods. As a young man, he'd had no choice *but* to keep his distance, when she read him like a blessed book. How he'd hated that. Every subtle expression, even the ones he worked to conceal, visible to her.

"Noah." Her teeth began to chatter, her breath chalking the air.

Wonderful. He shrugged from his coat and flung it over her shoulders, careful not to touch her.

He left her behind, rounding the corner of the house.

Elle huffed, struggling to match her stride to his, her hands fisted in his coat lapel. "The bottom floor is vacant, pretty much. Water damage. Needs repairs before it can be rented. Right now, I use the space for my school. Two classes a week. Tuesday and Thursday mornings. The typewriting machine *is* loud, but it shouldn't wake you."

He halted at the bottom of the staircase leading to the second-floor landing. So did she, her boots skidding across slick grass, her body, warm and soft, skidding into him. He set her back, trying to ignore the teasing scent of gingerbread and soap. *"School?* What could you teach a child? How to break an arm rolling off a roof? Better yet, how to shatter the largest pane of glass in town with a misplaced kick?"

He watched her swallow her first reply, the only time he remembered seeing her halt a foolish word from tumbling past those lovely lips of hers. "For your information, it's a school for *women.* Anyway, climbing the trellis was Caleb's idea. How was I to know the roof was still wet? And I worked all summer to replace that glass." She shivered, possibly more from indignation than chill, and gripped his coat close. The sleeves hung well past her wrists, the hem hitting her just above the knee. She appeared fragile and defenseless, a facade surely, yet Noah experienced the familiar compulsion to protect.

He took the stairs two at a time.

"It'll be quite cold in there until you get the parlor stove lit."

Parlor stove? Chrissakes, he hadn't seen a parlor stove in ten years, wasn't sure he would remember how to light one.

"If it's too chilly, you can come inside."

He glared over the railing. "I live in Chicago, Elle. In a printer's warehouse. If it gets above fifty in there, in July, I'll eat my hat. So, thank you anyway, but no need to worry."

"Fine, Professor. Freeze your skinny rump off."

He leaned out. "What did you say?"

"Nothing." She forced a smile, her lips clenched.

He couldn't halt his study of her, the little not hidden beneath his pilot coat. Reddish strands of hair curled about her face. Slim fingers locked around his lapel, pallid against the black wool. He denied the urge to squint, to see if her lashes were as long and dark as they had appeared up close. The absence of his spectacles and the misting rain painted a fanciful portrait. She even looked—*God help him*—attractive, her cheeks flushed, her eyes wide and very, very green.

Noah wrenched open the unlocked door, ducked inside, and slammed it behind him. Elle Beaumont was trouble and would never be anything *but* trouble. *Forget about how much it hurts to look at her and remember the life I left behind.*

Years ago, he had protected her from everyone, including herself. He wasn't going to do that again.

The woman was on her own this time.

OTHER BOOKS BY TRACY

GARRETT BROTHERS SERIES
Tides of Love
Tides of Passion
Tides of Desire: A Christmas Romance
(novella)

SOUTHERN HEAT SERIES
To Seduce a Rogue
To Desire a Scoundrel: A Christmas Seduction
(novella)

Coming February 2020
LEAGUE OF LORDS SERIES
The Lady is Trouble

Want more steamy historical romance reads?
Sign up for my mailing list
for giveaways and exclusive details on new
releases!

Follow me on Bookbub to check out what
romance reads I'm recommending!

ABOUT THE AUTHOR

TRACY'S STORY TELLING CAREER BEGAN when she picked up a copy of LaVyrle Spencer's *Vows* on a college beach trip. A journalism degree and a thousand romance novels later, she decided to try her hand at writing a southern version of the perfect love story. With a great deal of luck and more than a bit of perseverance, she sold her first novel to Kensington Publishing.

When not writing sensual stories featuring complex characters and lush settings, Tracy can be found reading romance, snowboarding, watching college football and figuring out how she can get to 100 countries before she kicks. She lives in the South, but after spending a few years in NYC, considers herself a New Yorker at heart.

Tracy has been awarded the National Reader's Choice, the Write Touch and the Beacon—with finalist nominations in the HOLT Medallion, Heart of Romance, Rising Stars and Reader's Choice. Her books have been translated into German, Dutch, Portuguese and Spanish. She loves hearing from readers about why she tends to pit her hero and heroine against each other from the very first page or that great romance she simply *must* read.

Sign up for my **Street Team** to read releases before they hit the shelves!

Or join my **newsletter** reader's group for exclusive giveaways and release information!

BookBub:
www.bookbub.com/profile/tracy-sumner
Twitter:
www.twitter.com/sumnertrac
Facebook:
www.facebook.com/Tracysumnerauthor

Made in the USA
Middletown, DE
30 November 2022

16537461R00097